# *Christmas in*
# Moonlight
# Falls

# Christmas in
# Moonlight Falls

## TRISH EVANS

StoneArch Bridge Books
Westlake Village, California

Christmas in Moonlight Falls: A Novella

Library of Congress Catalog Number: 2020916216
ISBN 978-1-7332349-3-1 (paperback)
ISBN 978-1-7332349-4-8 (epub) / 978-1-7332349-5-5 (mobi)

For more information visit
trishevansbooks.com

*For Michael*

God bless us, everyone.

~**Charles Dickens**
*A Christmas Carol*

May your strength give us strength
May your faith give us faith
May your hope give us hope
May your love give us love

~ Bruce Springsteen
*"Into the Fire"*

PART ONE

# LAST CHRISTMAS

# CHAPTER 1

DURING EACH OF the ten years since Annie Taylor had become Annie Morgan, she had always made Christmas the biggest, most important holiday of the year. But this year, Annie knew she had gone a little over the top with her decorations, summoning her competitive drive to deliver what she called her "personal best," both inside the house and outside. It was, after all, not just Christmas she would be celebrating on the 24th; it was also their tenth wedding anniversary. She and Ron had chosen Christmas Eve to tie the knot, knowing there would always be family around to help them celebrate, and for Annie it would always be one more reason to make the holidays even more special. So, when she began decorating the house on the Friday after Thanksgiving, well, one thing led to another and then to another. Ten wonderful years deserved something special.

"Are you sure you want to do that?" asked Ron, looking at the display of tiny white lights Annie had wrapped around every window in the living room.

"Just wait," said Annie. "*You're* going to love it." Annie folded a step ladder, held it parallel to the floor and started walking toward the kitchen. Annie Taylor Morgan had just turned thirty-two in

October and, thanks to hours at the gym and her own natural beauty, she had the kind of presence that made everyone take notice of her when she walked into a room. It didn't hurt that she was naturally blonde, stood just a shade under five-foot-nine and had a warm presence that honored others above herself.

"We're doing the kitchen next," said Emma to her dad, smiling proudly, ever her mom's loyal co-conspirator. Five years old, her long blonde hair tied back in a ponytail, Emma was a junior version of Annie—the same blue eyes, the same perfectly shaped face, the same smile, and the same built-in determination to reach a goal.

"Oh boy," said Ron. "I can't wait to see that one."

"*You're* going to love it," said Emma, echoing her mom's inflection.

"I already do," said Ron. "And if you need my help, just let me know." Even as he said the words, he knew what was coming next.

"Do you think you can finish the outside decorations today? It's supposed to snow tomorrow," said Annie. Boxes of Christmas lights and decorations were lined up in the garage like ships waiting in a harbor.

"I'll try," said Ron as he followed Annie into the kitchen. At thirty-five, Ron still had the chiseled, handsome look of a competitive downhill skier. Dressed in his standard winter weekend outfit of jeans and a flannel shirt, his long brown hair cascading just slightly over his collar, he had, by now, cultivated the image of a rugged outdoorsman who could also hold his own in a boardroom.

Pouring himself a glass of water, he glanced at Annie, who gave him a look that meant he'd better do more than try. "I'll get to it this afternoon, promise," said Ron as he gulped down the water, then walked from the kitchen toward a hallway leading to his office.

When it came to anything revolving around the house, Annie

could be a little head-strong, especially when momentary flashes of inspiration occurred—her frequent visions of what some area of the house "might be" or "could look like." When she drifted into one of those zones, Ron would usually retreat to his man-cave, a large den-like room where he had overseen the building of bookshelves made of aged pine stained in light oak to match the hardwood floors. On one side of the room, he'd placed a solid oak desk-table that held his computer and whatever project he was working on at the time. Behind the desk was a brown leather desk chair that reclined enough for Ron to lean back and put his feet up on the table. On the other side of the room was Ron's pride and joy, a 65" television screen mounted seamlessly on a white wall. Nearby, a Stickley leather sofa, so comfortable you'd never want to get up, had been placed behind a large wooden coffee table.

Ron plopped himself onto the sofa, rested his stocking-covered feet on the coffee table, and turned on the television to watch a college football game.

"Ron," Annie's voice called from the kitchen, "don't you dare start watching another football game. You have decorating to do!" Annie teased.

"Daddy, you have decorating to do!" Emma's giggle parroted her mother's order.

"Aye, aye, captains." Ron smiled with the warmth of a man who felt fully blessed by the love of his daughter and his wife. He often wondered how it was that he got so lucky. How was it possible that he, Ron Morgan, was able to find someone as amazing as Annie Taylor?

Ten years ago, as Annie was looking for her first job out of college, she had stumbled upon an online posting of a job at a Minneapolis marketing agency. On a lark, she posted her resume and the next thing Annie knew she was being interviewed by one of the owners, Ron Morgan, a recent Colorado transplant to the

Midwest. Ron had grown up in Darien, Connecticut, just outside of New York City, the son of a successful Madison Avenue advertising executive who had hoped his son would follow in his Yale footsteps and then join his agency. Instead, Ron needed to satisfy a son's desire to step outside a father's shadow, and when he was accepted to the University of Colorado in Boulder, he packed up his skis, hopped into his beat-up Jeep Wrangler and headed for the Rockies. Four years later, with a degree in anthropology, Ron and one of his ski-pals—a kid named Nate from Edina, Minnesota—formed Flatiron Sports Marketing, a company specializing in winter sports advertising and marketing. Their real motivation was to score free skiing passes at Arapahoe Basin or Breckenridge in exchange for advertising design work. The ploy succeeded, too, but the company sputtered for three years even as their modest start-up funds, a gift from their two fathers, dwindled. It looked like the party was over. Offered free rent from Nate's father back in Minnesota, the boys relocated from Boulder to Minneapolis and promptly landed a huge marketing contract with SportsGear, a booming outdoor sporting goods company.

Resuscitated by new cash flow, Flatiron Sports Marketing hired some bright recent college grads, including Annie Taylor, a recent valedictorian from St. Olaf College, who had impressed the two partners with her energy and intelligence. She was hired immediately as the new head of consumer research, a position for which she was woefully underqualified, having majored in English with a specialty in nineteenth century romantic literature. She could talk about the Brontë sisters all day but knew next to nothing about sports demographics, outdoor gear or consumer trends.

It didn't matter. Annie was smart, competitive and quick to absorb new information, and it took Ron about two minutes into the interview to know she would be a good hire and a great asset to the young company. What Ron didn't perceive at the time was that Annie knew a good man when she met one, and Ron Morgan was the absolute best man she had ever met. A few weeks after she was hired, Ron and Annie had begun meeting for morning coffee, which effortlessly evolved into business lunches and then dinners out after work. Annie and Ron tried to keep their various "meetings" undercover, but in a company of thirteen people, secrets were as transparent as the company budget—everyone knew Flatiron Sports Marketing was rolling in cash just like everyone knew Ron and Annie were an item. As their relationship flourished, so did the company, adding national contracts with a half dozen major sports manufacturers. They hired more people, expanded their office space, and as co-owner, Ron was suddenly making the kind of money he had never even imagined back when he and his partner Nate were bumming rides to Vail and begging for day passes on the slopes.

Ron took no time in proposing to Annie, and three months later, on Christmas Eve, they were married in the living room of the Taylor home in Moonlight Falls. The following year, with business booming, they had purchased a lot in the new Pikes Lake Country Club Estates just west of The Bluffs, a neighborhood that once was the town's premiere location overlooking the St. Croix River. Now, Pikes Lake was *the* place to live, and while Ron oversaw the company's continued growth, commuting to Flatiron's new offices in White Bear Lake, Annie oversaw the building of their dream home on a slight hill above Pike's Lake. No one was surprised.

"Daddy!"

Ron looked over his shoulder to see Emma standing in the doorway of his office with a fake frown on her face and her hands on her hips.

Ron laughed. "Did Mommy send you to spy on me?"

"You are in big trouble!"

Ron tiptoed to his daughter and began to tickle her tummy.

Emma giggled until she could take no more. It took a moment for her to catch her breath, but when she did, she put her finger to her lips.

Ron quickly responded, giving his daughter a solemn, expectant look.

"Mommy says you will be in deep trouble if you aren't already working on the outside decorations," whispered Emma.

"Then I'd better get going," Ron whispered. "Maybe after I finish, you and I can make our snowman."

"Snowgirl, Daddy!" Emma corrected him.

"Snowgirl!" Ron said as he lifted Emma high in the air and gave her a kiss on both cheeks.

"We can build her right next to the Emma Tree like we do every Christmas," said Emma as she clapped her hands with utter joy.

"That's exactly what we'll do as soon as I finish putting up the lights," said Ron, smiling at his daughter, knowing he would never forget a magical moment like this one, so simple, so pure, so filled with love and joy.

"Yay!" said Emma.

By the time Christmas Eve arrived that year, a round, sturdy snowgirl, wearing a red princess cape and red top hat, stood in the Morgan's front yard right alongside a five-year-old spruce tree. Both the tree and the snowgirl had been decorated with twinkling white lights, and behind them more strings of glowing white lights had been draped across the front porch, across the eves and along the surrounding dormer windows, giving the house a storybook glow.

Anyone standing outside the Morgan family's home on Pike's Lake could not help but feel the warmth and love and the spirit of Christmas.

# CHAPTER 2

ANNIE'S PARENTS, MOLLY and Bill Taylor, had lived in Moonlight Falls in an old Victorian house on Meadows Lane for thirty-five years. It's where they had raised their children and where the Taylor family had always gathered on both Christmas Eve and Christmas Day. With their standard decorations in place, both inside and out, Molly Taylor had been looking forward to *this* Christmas for a long time, even though they would desperately miss their son, Will, who was in his third deployment to Afghanistan. Molly felt particularly helpless about Will, knowing all she could do was pray for his safe return, which she did constantly, day and night, reciting a mantra to herself: *Please God, bring him home safe and sound.*

Dressed in a red Tartan plaid skirt and white lacy blouse, Molly, as always, looked much younger than her age, sixty-two. She would just roll her eyes when Bill would tell her she didn't look a day over forty, but it was true. Her shoulder length hair, a blend of natural blonde and natural white hair, had never known dye of any kind.

As Molly went through her usual Christmas Eve preparations, she was aware of how fortunate she was that her other two children, Annie and Jenny, were both living within ten minutes of her, right here in Moonlight Falls. No airplane tickets needed, no worries about travel, weather, or being stuck in some distant corner of America. They were both right here in the neighborhood, both happily married, both able to spend time with Molly and Bill and able to help in any way, if needed. Even during Molly's darkest moments, when she had worried about Will and the extremely dangerous situations he no doubt faced every day, she had always pushed those negative thoughts aside and focused on tomorrow, envisioning new events, maybe even new grandchildren to hug and hold. That had always been her way, and she saw no reason to change.

Molly often thought that their Queen Anne-styled house, which dated back to the 1880s, looked best with a dusting of snow on the roof and strands of white Christmas lights twinkling above the front porch. *There is just something about our home,* she thought to herself that Christmas Eve Day as she moved from the living room to the dining room and then to the kitchen; every corner was filled with wonderful memories of raising their three children here.

Inside, Christmas music played on built-in speakers throughout the house, and the glorious scents of Molly's Christmas cuisine were wafting from the kitchen, where a large roast was cooking in the oven. With a nod to her Scandinavian roots, Molly had prepared something called *fruktsoppa* in Swedish but known in their household as "froo-ta-soopa," a hair-raising concoction of dried fruits, sugar, cinnamon and various juices cooked on a low flame for most of a day, then served hot as an appetizer or cold as dessert. A little went a long way.

"Mmmm, smells good in here," Bill Taylor said from the mud room near the back door while shaking snow off his parka and slipping out of his winter boots. He hung the coat on a hook and entered the kitchen, blowing on his hands to warm them up. A handsome man in his mid-60s, Bill's face was flushed crimson as a result of spending the last forty-five minutes shoveling snow. "Have you looked outside? It's really coming down," said Bill, looking out the side window. "I shoveled the front steps, and when I finished, I had to start all over again." He stepped closer to Molly who was hovering near the range. "Just give me a little taste."

Molly stirred the soup and then handed a large spoonful to Bill. "Careful, it's hot," she warned. Bill blew once on the spoon, then sipped.

"Ooooff-ta," he said, intentionally using an all-purpose Minnesota expression while squinting at the sweet and sour taste.

Molly smiled at the compliment.

"Please Sir, I want some more?" he said, his phony English accent echoing the words of Oliver Twist. Bill's terrible imitations had been a running gag for decades, but Molly always laughed at them anyway. He dipped the spoon back into the soup.

"That's enough," said Molly. "You'd better get ready. Jenny called and they're on their way." She looked at the clock on the kitchen wall, which showed it was nearly 3:45. "And Annie, Emma and Ron will be here any minute."

He put the spoon back in the fruit soup. "I'll be baaack," he said in a lame imitation of Arnold Schwarzenegger.

Molly giggled as she shushed her husband out of the kitchen.

Pausing for a second to drink in the joyous sight of Emma's tree and Ron and Emma's snowgirl, Annie, with an armful of Christmas packages, nearly slipped on the snowy sidewalk. She quickly regained her footing, shuffled to the trunk of their SUV and stashed the gifts inside. Carefully, she turned and hurried back into the house, her hair now covered in fresh snow.

"Here's some more, Mommy." Emma held three wrapped gifts in her arms. One larger present sat on the floor behind the couch.

"Thank you, sweetie." Then, with a silly grin, Annie teased her five-year-old daughter with an obvious question. "But what about the big box behind you?"

Emma looked at the box. "Oh, yeah. Well, it's so big that I was thinking… maybe I should open it now." A pretty good conniver, Emma looked at her mom with a pleading face.

"No way, you silly girl. You know the tradition. Everyone gets to open just one Secret Santa gift at Grandma and Grandpa's house tonight."

"But I really want to open it now. I just know it's Wella." Wella was Emma's favorite American Doll, because, like Wella, Emma was outdoorsy and loved discovering new plants and animals in her garden. Emma knew she was not going to persuade her mom, but she thought it was worth a try.

"I'll tell you what, if you put on your snow boots and your jacket, I'll let you carry your present to the car. That way you can shake it before you put it in the trunk. Okay?"

Emma's eyes lit up as she pulled on her jacket and her fur-lined hunter green wellies, the same ones that Wella wore.

"Ron, we're going to be late!" yelled Annie up the stairway.

Ron had been upstairs frantically trying to wrap the diamond earrings he had bought for Annie. He knew he'd gone a little overboard on this gift but, hey, he and Annie were also celebrating ten years of a beautiful marriage *that night*. Ron seemed to be all thumbs, bungling the gift wrapping, Scotch tape sticking to his fingers and crinkling the paper. Finally, he just wrapped a few layers of ribbon around the small box, put a big red bow in the center and grabbed his coat.

"I'll be right down," yelled Ron as he stuffed the gift inside the coat pocket and dashed down the stairway.

When he reached the bottom step, he threw his arms out to his sides and said, "Ta-da!"

Both Annie and Emma laughed out loud at what they saw. Ron was wearing a bright red wool sweater, a pair of bright green corduroy slacks and a green elf hat with large elf ears flapping on each side of his head.

Annie and Emma ran over to give him a group hug.

"Am I Christmas-ee enough for you?" said Ron, happy to be received so lovingly.

"Daddy, you look like a giant elf!" said Emma, giggling.

"I am an elf, and I've got surprises from Santa just for you," said Ron, putting his arms around Annie and Emma's shoulders to escort them out the front door. "C'mon, we don't want to be late!"

Bill and Molly were seated side by side on a sofa in their living room, an icy tension hanging in the air. The Christmas music had been turned down low and the once blazing fire had smoldered into dying embers, burning quietly in the brick fireplace. Wearing a bulky, green-tinged sweater, Jenny was seated on the floor, next to the fireplace leaning against the legs of her husband, Sam, who was seated on a stuffy, leather chair. An attorney by day and always comfortable in business attire, Sam was wearing a red vest, a red bow tie and a white shirt, looking a little overdressed but very comfortable in the living room of his in-laws.

"Should I try calling her again?" asked Molly, looking at her husband.

"You've called three times. Maybe they got stuck in the snow," said Bill. "You know Ron. He likes to plow right through everything."

"She would have called," said Molly, getting more worried by the moment.

From outside, they heard the sound of a car door. "At last," said Bill. Both Bill and Molly stood up and rushed to the front door to greet Annie, Emma and Ron.

The instant Bill opened the door, he knew something terrible had happened. Two young police officers were standing on the front porch, both wearing grim, foreboding looks on their faces.

"Mr. Taylor?"

"Yes," said Bill.

"My name is Officer Adamson," said the older one. "This is Officer Ashley."

"What's going on?" said Bill urgently. Molly, Jenny and Sam were now standing behind him.

"There's been an accident."

"Oh my God," said Molly, putting her hands to her face. "Are they okay?"

"No, I'm afraid not," said Officer Adamson. "I'm sorry, but the accident took the life of Ron Morgan. His wife—"

"Annie?" screeched Molly, horrified.

"Mrs. Morgan is on the way to Valley Medical Center."

"What about Emma… our granddaughter?" Bill was trying to hold back his fear.

"I can tell you that your granddaughter is also *en route* to the hospital."

"Oh my God," said Molly, reeling backwards, in shock. Sam and Jenny both tried to steady her.

"What happened?" asked Bill, wanting the details but not sure he wanted to hear them in front of his wife and daughter.

"With the snow and ice, it appears that the SUV driven by Mr. Morgan lost control coming down the steep hill from the Bluffs," said Officer Ashley. He was articulate and compassionate at the same time. "Unfortunately, the SUV slid right onto Main Street just as a snowplow was approaching the intersection." He stopped to let his audience fill in the details for themselves.

"Oh my God, oh my God, Bill. Poor Ron. We need to, oh no, oh my God—" said Molly, stammering. She turned to her husband who hugged her tightly, letting her nestle her head into his chest.

"I'm here," whispered Bill to his wife.

"Oh, God, why?" Molly began to shake and sob uncontrollably.

PART TWO

# CHRISTMAS THIS YEAR

# CHAPTER 3

IN YEARS PAST, Annie had always begun decorating for Christmas the day after Thanksgiving. But not this year. Not after all she'd been through in the last eleven months. Annie was just not up to celebrating Christmas. Oh, she loved her family dearly and had always loved Christmas more than anyone. But since the car accident last December that had killed her husband and left her six-year-old daughter in a wheelchair, Annie just did not have it in her to be festive and jolly. She needed a distraction from last year and from Christmas memories in general.

Staring out the front window of the home she and Ron had built eight years ago in the Pike's Lake Estates, Annie watched the snow pile up on the boughs of pine trees and remembered how Ron and Emma had rolled three wet, compacted snow balls and then piled them on top of each other to build Emma's snowgirl in their front yard, complete with the fur lined princess cape and top hat. Ron had a spotlight trained on their snowgirl so that no one driving past their house could miss it.

Annie turned and walked from the living room back to the kitchen, where Emma had rolled her wheelchair to the refrigerator and was staring at the calendar taped to the refrigerator door.

"Mommy, tell me again. How many days until we fly to Orlando?" asked Emma.

"Let's see," said Annie, leaning over Emma's shoulder to look at the calendar. "It looks like exactly twenty-seven days from today!"

"Ohhh, that's so long to wait." Emma frowned at the calendar, then rolled her wheelchair away from the refrigerator so she wouldn't have to stare at the empty days ahead.

Originally, Emma had not loved the idea of spending Christmas away from her grandparents and Aunt Jenny and Uncle Sam. She had even overheard her grandmother say something about Uncle Will maybe coming home for Christmas. When she asked her mom later that night, Annie told her she just didn't know. "Is he okay?" Emma had pressed her. Annie assured her daughter that Uncle Will was okay, but no one knew if he would make it home by Christmas. In the same conversation, Annie had proposed that the two of them could have their own special Christmas in Orlando, Florida, away from the biting cold of Minnesota. "A week of fun in the sun," was how Annie had pitched it to her daughter.

There were times, Annie had noticed, when Emma would become pensive and thoughtful, retreating into her own world to think or contemplate something. This was one of those times. A few days later, while they were sitting down to have dinner, Emma sat up straight in her wheelchair and, before touching her food, announced that she had something important to say. "I've been thinking about Christmas in Florida," she said, then waited for a moment just to keep her mother in suspense.

"And...?"

"And I think it would be awesome!"

"All right! Let's do it!" said Annie with a big smile, holding out her right hand for a high-five. *Smack!*

Packing for the big trip had begun right after Thanksgiving, even though the flight was almost a month away.

Part of Annie's motivation for the trip had been to avoid facing the memory of Christmas Eve one year ago when instead of basking in the love of Christmas spirit at her parents' home, she had spent last Christmas Eve in the E.R., fearing for her daughter's life while trying to absorb the shock of losing her husband. This year would be the first "new normal" Christmas, as some well-wishers had called it. Annie hated that term, new normal. *How dare anyone say that to her.* There was nothing normal about what had happened or what she and Emma faced. She hated the thought that this would be her first Christmas Eve wedding anniversary where Ron would not be there by her side. If she stayed at home in Moonlight Falls this year, it would only amplify her loss and her loneliness, so Annie had hoped her parents and siblings would understand when she told everyone about her holiday plans for this Christmas.

Molly, Bill and Jenny all voiced their approval, but Annie could tell by the way they looked and by the sound of their voices that they were just paying lip service to her and that behind their supportive and kindhearted words was an unspoken inference: *Shouldn't you and Emma be with your family and not be alone at a time like this?*

Annie's cell phone rang and she saw MOM on the caller I.D.

"Hi Mom," answered Annie, knowing today was a chemo-day for her mother. Earlier that year, Molly had received a startling diagnosis. Breast cancer.

"Hi Honey." Molly Taylor was seated in the driver's seat of her Jeep Grand Cherokee, parked in the open-air parking ramp of a new medical center about twenty miles west of Moonlight Falls near White Bear Lake. The car was warming up and Molly was staring out the front window watching the snow, which at that moment was coming down very hard.

"How did your therapy go?" Annie asked, her voice sounding a little reedy through the car's speaker system.

"Just finished."

Molly would need to complete one more infusion of chemotherapy before knowing if the cancer had been obliterated. Much to her surprise, the process had not been as difficult an ordeal as she had expected. One infusion every three weeks would leave her tired, sometimes nauseous, and, of course, she had gone bald, but all in all, Molly had been able to perform most of the daily tasks she'd done before the treatments began.

"Did the doctor say how your numbers are?" Annie worried about her mother's health on an ongoing basis and did what she could to help out. She and Emma often bought precooked casseroles and stews from a nearby family run restaurant and took them to her parents' house during chemo weeks.

"No, but you know how that goes. I probably won't know anything definite until after the holidays." Molly paused briefly. "Annie, there's another reason I called."

"What's that?"

Molly hesitated... only because she felt guilty for what she was about to ask of her daughter. She knew and understood the pain Annie had endured over the past months and truly appreciated why this Christmas would be especially hard for her and Emma. Molly adjusted the knitted stocking cap that covered her bald head. "I know you're bent on taking the trip to Florida, but, well, honey, a complication has suddenly come up, and I thought I should let you know before you and Emma finalize your flight plans for Orlando."

Annie braced herself for another one of her mother's thinly disguised pleas to have Christmas at the family home. "Mom, you do know we have our plane tickets, right?"

"Yes... well, dear, it seems that someone has made an offer to buy our house. It's a very good offer, and, well, the truth of the matter is your father and I have decided to accept it."

"What?" Annie was stunned. Her mind raced ahead as if she were on caffeine. *Why would her parents even contemplate selling the family home—the home that she and her brother and sister had grown up in? The only home Molly and Bill had ever owned? The home where all the happy and wonderful and, yes, even painful memories of the Taylor family had occurred. Why now?*

"I know it's a shock, but it just sort of happened."

It bothered Annie that her mother sounded chipper while telling her this upsetting news. "Mom, how does something like that just sort of happen? Are you leaving Moonlight Falls? Where are you going? And why didn't you tell me?" Whenever she was nervous or excited, Annie talked fast, her voice grew louder and the tempo became more impatient. The tone of Annie's voice carried the firm message that she felt betrayed. *Hadn't she lost enough over the past months?*

"It happened kind of fast, but a nice young couple knocked on our door a few weeks ago and asked if we were interested in selling the house. They said they'd always dreamed of living in Moonlight Falls in a home just like ours. Of course, your dad told them the house wasn't for sale and that we weren't even contemplating such a thing. But then the husband handed Dad his card and wanted us to contact him if we ever decided to sell and, well, it kind of got us thinking about downsizing, and… I don't know, we can't live in such a big home forever."

"But Mom—" Annie was shaken.

"Now don't worry, Annie, we're not moving until after the New Year, so that gives us almost two months to get everything in order and…." She paused for a moment, collecting her thoughts. "And it will give everyone one last Christmas together in the family home."

Emma had wheeled her chair back in front of the refrigerator, where she was tapping on the calendar with her finger, counting out loud the number of days left before December twenty-fourth. "Six, seven, eight, nine…"

Annie stepped out of the kitchen and into the dining room so Emma could not hear her.

"Oh, Mom, Emma is so excited about the vacation," she said quietly. "It will break her heart if we don't go. And… I just don't want her to be reminded of last Christmas."

"Annie, I promise we'll make it a very special time, one that will help heal the memory of last Christmas for you and Emma and," she paused, "for the whole family."

"I don't know." Annie walked from the dining room to the living room, where she sat on a sofa and looked out the window. It had started snowing an hour earlier and now it was coming down with a vengeance.

Across the street Annie saw that many of her neighbors' houses were already trimmed with colorful lights and adorned with cheery signs—one pointing to the North Pole, another saying simply, PEACE, and still another flashing off and on "Merry" then "Christmas." Even though Annie had determined a few weeks ago that these decorations were simply a visual version of white noise, it was another reason she wanted to get away. There was just too much Christmas here. Plus, Annie had neither the desire nor the energy to decorate her own home inside the way she always did, or outside the way Ron had done every year of their marriage.

"I imagine Jenny and Will are just as shocked as I am," said Annie.

"Actually, I haven't spoken to them yet," said Molly. "I wanted to call you first. In case you decided to change your plans."

"Let me think about it," Annie said rather coldly. She did not like the position her mother had put her in with this change. Nor did she think selling the family home was the right next step for her parents. She couldn't fathom them leaving the old house on Meadows Lane.

"Dad and I will pay for all the change fees, if that will help," said Molly, hoping her offer would not insult her daughter.

Molly's offer was met with silence on the other end of the phone line. Annie finally responded. "Thanks, Mom. Um, I'm still in shock over this. I'll get back to you later."

Annie clicked off her phone and turned away from the window.

# CHAPTER 4

THE SNOW HAD let up for the moment, but a fresh covering of five or six inches had given the Taylor's well-kept Victorian house a cheery accent to the twinkling Christmas lights framing the front porch and the roofline along the front and the dormers of the second story. A yet-to-be-decorated Christmas tree was visible through the living room window, just like in nearly every house on Meadows Lane. Their street, Molly always thought, was the quaintest of the dozens of quaint residential streets in the charming Meadows neighborhood of Moonlight Falls.

The garage was tucked behind the Taylor's house, reachable by a long driveway on the left side of the house that turned into icy ruts in the winter and slush in the spring. With their son Will no longer at home, responsibility for shoveling the driveway had reverted to Bill, who in turn, hired a high school kid from down the street to shovel as needed for twenty bucks a time. He turned out to be somewhat unreliable, which meant Bill and Molly often parked their cars behind each other in the narrow driveway near the street and then begged each other to move whichever car was blocking the other. The ritual had become their winter dance, although the valet work more often fell to Bill.

Dressed in a down vest and comfortable weekend clothes, Bill Taylor was in the garage sifting through boxes of Christmas decorations while nearby, a small herd of wire-framed reindeer waited to be deployed to the front yard. Bill plugged in their power cords one at a time and watched with satisfaction as each of the reindeer lighted up.

Next, Bill picked up two plastic toy soldiers and, carrying one under each arm, he stepped outside the garage and trudged toward the front of the house, stumbling on some hidden ice ruts as snowflakes landed softly on his wavy, gray hair. *It's just a house,* Bill was thinking. *But oh, if these walls could talk… what stories they would tell.* From the first baby crying in the middle of the night to dinner table conversations to the tears shed when eighteen-year-old Will left for Army boot camp, this drafty old nineteenth century home had seen a whole lot of love… and yes, some sorrow, too, but mostly love and happiness. And now Bill was thinking that it was time to leave, *time to move on.* He reached the front steps and set a toy soldier down on either side, wrested them each into place through piles of shoveled snow, then plugged each one into a waiting extension cord. He stepped back and admired them, as if welcoming a couple of old pals, pleased to see the glowing soldiers standing firm and resolute, once more in service to the Taylor home.

Molly wove her black Grand Cherokee SUV north along River Road and then turned left onto Meadows Lane, the street on which she and Bill had lived happily for so many years. As December's early dusk settled in, Molly drove slowly so she could take a long look at each of the decorated homes along the way. She knew every family in every home, some better than others, and while she would never admit it publicly, there was always a little competition between the neighbors to see who had the best decorations, who had the most charming house, who had oldest Victorian, and so on. She smiled just thinking about how ridiculous that competition was and how good it felt to be driving on her street and to see the warm glow and twinkling lights emanating from each of the homes even as Christmas carols floated from her car radio, a welcome musical distraction from the nagging feeling within her belly.

Wheeling her car into the driveway of her house, Molly smiled when she saw the three wire reindeer perfectly placed near the two birch trees, their white lights twinkling in the dusk, and the two steadfast toy soldiers, durable sentries once again standing guard on the front steps.

Molly found Bill in the garage workshop busily working on a gift he'd been building for Emma—a dollhouse with an especially large swinging door, finally starting to take shape.

"It's beautiful, Bill," said Molly.

Bill turned and looked at his wife. "Getting there. Hope Emma will like it. You know, there's something to be said for building a gift from scratch with my own hands. Especially for Emma. Takes me back to when the kids were young." Even as he got the words out, Bill was reading Molly's mood like a book, immediately sensing something was wrong.

Molly stood beside her husband and quietly examined Emma's Christmas gift.

"She's going to love it."

"The one thing I'm going to miss for sure is my workshop," said Bill. He looked around at the plethora of woodworking tools, trappings from a lifetime of puttering and building. "What am I going to do with all of this stuff?"

"I don't know, dear." Molly sighed, wondering, as she often

did, how her husband could stand all the clutter she was seeing. "But you really don't use it as much as you used to."

"I guess…" He wanted to say something more, but the words wouldn't come.

Bill Taylor was the founder and owner of a public relations company with offices on the east side of St. Paul, only thirty-some miles away. Over the years, he had attracted more than enough clients to build a thriving business, and he loved every part of it. As Molly knew all too well, he was much more capable of crafting a press release than building a dollhouse, but he had picked up some carpentry skills from his dad, an engineer, and he liked woodworking, maybe for the solitude of the task in stark contrast to the intense, daily interaction with people, a fact of business life in his chosen career. Lately, he had scaled back his work schedule, mainly to be sure he was around to help Molly on the days she was feeling weak from chemotherapy. She had been a real trouper throughout the entire ordeal, and even though she did not need or demand any extra attention, Bill wanted to stay close to home, which more often than not led him to his garage workshop, where he would tinker in the good company of the woodworking tools he'd inherited and that still bore the carved initials of his father and grandfather.

Bill put his arm around Molly's shoulders. "How did your treatment go today?"

"Oh, fine. You know how it is. The doctor doesn't have any more information about whether or not the chemo is working. Not until after the last treatment."

Molly had finished four months of chemotherapy treatments, and after today's treatment, she had just one more—one last session just two weeks before Christmas. She wouldn't know if the chemo had killed all the breast cancer cells until after Christmas.

"By the way, I called Annie on my way home and told her about the house."

"How'd *that* go?"

Molly tilted her head and replied, "She was shocked, of course."

"I'm sure. Is there any chance they'll stay in town for Christmas?"

"She said she'd think about it, but I'm doubtful. Emma's heart is set on going to Orlando," said Molly. "Annie's had such a hard time this year—she's just hopeful that being away in Florida will keep them from reliving the memory of last Christmas."

"At least she didn't say no right away." Bill loved his oldest daughter and felt her pain but was also very proud of her for the manner in which she'd pulled through during the last eleven months. Of course, Bill knew she would. Of the three children, he had always felt Annie was the toughest, emotionally and intellectually. Annie had always been a Type-A person—straight A's all through high school and college, then a high-powered marketing job, where she helped catapult the company to national prominence... and fell in love with her boss. It was no surprise when Annie and Ron bought a spectacular "starter" home near the country club, close enough for Ron to commute to his office, but far enough from all the construction and hubbub at home. Annie and Ron loved their home even more because they had supervised the building of it themselves and then, with the help of an interior designer and a landscape architect, had it exquisitely decorated inside and expertly landscaped outside. When Emma was born, Annie had hired the most qualified nanny (from the most elite nanny agency) who helped out until Emma began school at the most prestigious nursery school, followed by elementary school at the revered West Moonlight Falls Academy.

"They're certainly on a different path than we were," Molly once said to Bill late at night after attending Grandparent's Day at

Emma's preschool. "But maybe it's the right one for them." Molly remembered that Bill had nodded quietly, usually his way of disagreeing but not wanting to ruffle anyone's feathers.

After the accident, many of Annie's Type-A tendencies had simply disappeared. She was no longer as fastidious about her house nor as concerned with her appearance as she once had been, no longer wearing makeup or her designer clothes. Most days she chose to don a T-shirt and jeans with sneakers, and in place of going to her hairdresser twice a month, Annie had let her hair grow long, often pulling it back into a simple ponytail or bun. The beautiful house with its eco-friendly landscaping, of which she and Ron had been so proud, took on a tired, less "manicured" appearance, as if it, too, could not shake the sadness of loss.

The only area of life where Annie had taken charge in her typical Type-A manner had to do with Emma. Annie had kept her position at Flatiron Creative, but insisted that she work from home, thereby giving her more time to spend with Emma. Annie made sure Emma had the finest physical therapists even if it meant driving ninety minutes to and from the therapist's office at the University of Minnesota. Annie had also dedicated herself to home schooling Emma so as to allow the flexibility needed for doctor appointments and therapy sessions.

"You're right, at least she didn't say no." Molly squeezed Bill's hand as they walked through the snow toward the back door of the house. "I'd better call Jenny before she finds out from Annie."

"Let's just make sure Jenny and Sam still plan to be home for Christmas," Bill said. "Hopefully, Will can get here, too." He watched as Molly slowly walked up the three steps to the back porch. It pained him to see how several months of chemo had slowed his once lively and energetic wife.

# CHAPTER 5

SEATED AT HER kitchen table, a cordless phone in front of her, Molly had dreaded calling Jenny, her second-oldest child, with the news about the planned sale of the family home. Of her three children, Jenny loved the two-story Victorian the most and even as a young child she would complain any time Molly had the audacity to replace a carpet or change a window treatment. Ironically, Jenny became an interior decorator and, even so, it was Jenny who a few years back complained when Molly and Bill decided to add a breakfast nook to their kitchen and expand the tiny family room. They just wanted to enlarge the space where everyone always gathered, rationalizing that one day in the not-too-distant future, there would be grandchildren running through the hallways. Annie was pregnant with Emma at the time, and Molly and Bill explained to Jenny how they just wanted to be prepared for an ever-growing family—who knew how many grandchildren would fill the Taylors' kitchen and family room? At the time, Jenny was engaged to Sam, and they had hoped to start a family soon after they were married. After stewing over the idea for a few days, Jenny withdrew her objections, but only under the condition that Molly include Jenny in all of their decision making. Jenny did not want some misguided architect foisting his opinion onto her parents, leading them toward one of those cold and sterile mid-century interiors, the kind her sister Annie loved. That just wouldn't be right.

Privately, Molly and Bill often shook their heads, wondering how they somehow managed to breed two Type-A kids, and both of them girls, with such contrasting personalities. Strangely, Annie had become more laid back in the months since Ron's death, and so had Jenny. It was almost as if an osmosis between the two girls had taken place, a transference or merging of personalities between the two of them. The fact that Jenny and Sam had had five miscarriages in the six years since they had gotten married may also have contributed to Jenny's newfound reserve, especially when facing life's decisions. Molly worried about her middle child, who was clearly struggling with the possibility that she might never be able to carry a pregnancy to term.

"Hi, Mom," answered Jenny. Her voice sounded worried. "How did it go today? Are you feeling okay?" Jenny was at her office at the design company, and when the call came in from her mom, she walked across the room and closed the door.

"I feel fine, sweetie. It's always the first few days after chemo that I feel tired and nauseous. I'm going to take it easy for the rest of the week."

"Good. Can I bring you something for dinner tonight?"

"No, no. I bought some chicken pot pies on my way home," Molly said, bracing herself to tell Jenny the reason for the call.

"Well, eat as much as you can, okay, Mom?" While wrapped with love, this was a firm, no-nonsense order, in keeping with Jenny's personality—firm, direct and imposing.

In contrast to her tall, blonde-haired, blue-eyed sister, Jenny was short, just over five-feet five-inches tall, with dark hair and steely-brown eyes that gave her a more serious disposition than anyone else in the family. While Annie had channeled her academic energy into reading literature and creative writing, Jenny had always been able to draw, a skill she learned from Molly who had, as a teenager, done some cheery watercolor paintings. Always an enthusiastic student, Jenny effortlessly delivered a 4.0 grade average and knew from an early age that she would be able to parlay her artistic abilities into a career.

Jenny and her husband, Sam, had grown up together, attending Moonlight Falls Elementary, then River Valley Consolidated High School, graduating in the same class, then both attending "the U" where Sam majored in political science and went right on to law school. Jenny took her degree in interior design and began working for a Minneapolis design firm while Sam finished law school. To no one's surprise, neither Sam nor Jenny ever wanted to date anyone else, nor did they want to live anywhere other than Moonlight Falls. This was their hometown and would be the hometown of the children they planned on having just as soon as they were married. "We're going to have lots and lots of children," Jenny would say to Sam, after which, Sam would tease, "Does that mean three or twenty-three?"

So, soon after Sam finished law school, he and Jenny were married and, with a little help from Sam's father, they bought a small, three-bedroom cottage in the Old Town neighborhood, a few blocks from the river. The homes in Old Town were quaint, 1930's two-story Folk Victorians that had gone through a period of neglect until young couples like Jenny and Sam started buying and renovating them.

"Mom, I'm worried that you're not getting enough nutrition," said Jenny. She knew she was on the edge of being annoying, but wanted to be sure her mom listened, too.

Chemo had always left Molly without an appetite, and Jenny was worried that her mother would most likely take a measly bite or two of her dinner and leave the rest on her plate. This past year had left Jenny with a long list of things to worry about: the car accident that killed Annie's husband; Emma's physical challenges of being wheelchair bound with only the slimmest hope of eventually gaining enough strength to walk again; Annie's struggle to make life work without her husband; Molly's breast cancer battle; Will's well-being in Afghanistan; and, yes, the anxiety and apprehension she and Sam were both feeling these last two months.

In September, when Jenny had once again become pregnant, this for the sixth time, she and Sam had decided not to mention it to anyone—it would only add to everyone's stress and worries, especially since the odds of another miscarriage were too high. Jenny and Sam quietly kept the information to themselves, determined to wait, as her obstetrician had suggested, until the baby was past the third-month gestation period, which would be just a week before Christmas. If she didn't have a miscarriage by then, well, she and Sam would let the family know.

"Jenn, dear, there's a reason I called," said Molly, her voice sounding weak and hesitant.

"Oh, Mom." Jenny sighed heavily, expecting bad news regarding Molly's cancer numbers. She had dreaded this moment every single day.

"It's not bad news, Jenny," said Molly, reacting to the fear in her daughter's voice.

"Oh... oh, thank goodness!" Jenny exhaled, then sat down at her desk.

"Actually, it's good news. You see, your father and I received an outstanding offer from a very nice young couple, and we've decided to take it."

"An offer on what? Your car?" asked Jenny, her voice rising.

"No, no. An offer on, well, um, on the house." Molly braced

herself for Jenny's characteristically melodramatic reaction to any news regarding change.

"You what?" Jenny jumped up from her chair. "Mom, you're kidding, aren't you?"

"No, sweetie, I'm not." Molly had a lump in her throat, even though she had anticipated this reaction from Jenny.

"But why? Mom, that's your home. You love it. Dad loves it. Annie and Will and I love it! It's not just yours and Dad's home. It is our home, too!" Jenny began pacing the floor, building herself into a frenzy of emotion.

"Jenny, listen to me. It just seems to be the right time for Dad and me."

Jenny could hear the pain in Molly's voice and immediately realized that maybe her mother's illness was the reason for what seemed to be such a reckless decision. Normally, Jenny would have begged and pleaded with her mother and father until they changed their minds, but hearing the pain in her mother's voice, she realized that most likely the cancer had caused her parents to face an unknown future... the possibility of...

Jenny pushed the thought away and regained control of her emotions. "Mom, this makes me so sad, but I guess I should be happy for you, right? I'm sure this wasn't an easy decision for you and Dad."

Molly was stunned at Jenny's reaction. There were no hysterics or theatrics behind her words. Just a sudden, mature forfeiting of her own opinion on the matter. This most certainly was not the Jenny she thought she knew.

"Thank you, Jenny, for understanding." All the tension in Molly's body had melted away. "The good news is we won't move until after January first, so our whole family can have one last Christmas at home."

"Well, that's good." Jenny was trying very hard to digest the alarming news without upsetting her mother. "That's great, except Mom, the whole family won't be home. Annie and Emma will be in Orlando. And we don't know for sure about Will."

"I spoke with Annie earlier today."

"Did she say they'd be home for Christmas?" Jenny was hopeful.

"No, she said she'd think about it," said Molly, with doubt in her voice. "And I certainly understand how being home for Christmas might be too hard on her."

"Let me talk to Annie. We've all got to be together this Christmas, especially if it's going to be our last one on Meadows Lane," said Jenny. "We can't erase what happened last Christmas Eve, but we can't let it be the final one we all share in our home."

# CHAPTER 6

WILLIAM TAYLOR, JR., called Will by everyone except his sisters, who had persisted in calling him Willy even into his teenage years, was the youngest of Molly and Bill's three children and looked very much like a junior version of his father. His once thick head of wavy black hair had now been trimmed to stubble by a military barber, but he had his dad's thick shoulders and the same bright eyes, quick sense of humor and confident charm. As a child, Will had been laid-back and even-tempered, unbothered by anything. While his family thought of him as easygoing, he had also been a standout defensive back at Valley High School, fast, hard-hitting and good enough to be offered several NCAA Division-1 football scholarships, all of which he declined in order to fulfill a childhood dream of joining the United States Army.

Military service had turned Will into a muscular, intense young man, one who was committed to the Army and who, in turn, had earned the respect of his peers and his commanding officers. In short, he was a soldier's soldier, now in the final month of his third deployment to Afghanistan, this time in Kandahar Province, a Taliban stronghold in the most troubled region of a very troubled country.

In the middle of September, while out on a reconnaissance mission on a remote road that led seemingly to nowhere, a bomb had exploded near where Will had been walking, plastering his knees with shrapnel and severely injuring his left leg.

The first telephone call to the Taylors had come early one morning, a week after the bomb had detonated, from a military hospital in Wiesbaden, Germany, where Will had been airlifted for surgery. His rehabilitation had already begun, and he had sounded in good spirits.

"I'll be okay," Will had said during that early morning call to his parents, a few days after his first surgery. "It's nothing, really. But I'll be rehabbing for a month or so over here."

"We'd like to come and visit," said Molly as tears welled up in her eyes.

"No, there's no need. It's really nothing, Mom. Doc says I'll be stateside before too long. I might even get home for Christmas."

Will had made it sound like he'd gotten no more than a scratch on his leg, the physical equivalent of a headache. *Take an aspirin and get some rest.* His parents both knew there was probably more to it, but Will was just being Will—the football player who never missed a game despite broken fingers, sprained knees and a few minor concussions.

*There was nothing to worry about,* Bill and Molly had kept telling themselves in the days after that phone call with their son. Privately, they were extremely worried. Several times, Bill noticed Molly staring off into space, as if trying to connect with her son by channeling some sort of psychic telepathy. As for Bill, he found himself waking up in the middle of the night, unable to sleep, in which case he would retreat to his office and sometimes dash off a quick email to Will in hopes of getting more information or just a reassurance that he was doing okay.

Now here it was, a few weeks before Christmas, three months

after the roadside explosion, and they still did not know if Will would make it home for Christmas. Molly had just finished speaking to Jenny and was about to leave the kitchen to tell Bill how Jenny had taken the news of the house sale, when her cell phone rang. She looked at the phone and was surprised to see Will's caller I.D.

"Will!" Molly almost squealed.

"Hey, Mom." Will's voice was as cheerful as ever. "What's up?"

"Oh, Will, it's so good to hear your voice."

"Looks like I'll be home before Christmas and—"

"Oh, thank goodness! I was worried you were calling to say you wouldn't be coming home after all."

"What? And miss Christmas in Moonlight Falls? No way!"

"Oh, I'm so happy to hear that, Will. Where are you?"

"Walter Reed Hospital in Bethesda, Maryland. The docs here have been great. I'm just about good as new."

"Oh, Willy. That's such wonderful news. We've been thinking about you every day."

"I can't wait to get home."

Molly hesitated for a moment. She hadn't planned to tell Will about the house sale until they could tell him in person, but now that he was on the phone, she decided it was best to bring him into the conversation.

"Your dad and I have some news to share with you."

"I'm going to be an uncle again?" asked Will, jumping to an obvious conclusion. He knew how much Jenny and Sam had wanted a child.

"Oh, well, no, at least not that I know of," said Molly. She paused, searching for just the right words. "Your dad and I have found a buyer for the house, and we've decided to sell."

"Wow, that is news," said Will. "I guess you'll be cleaning

out my room, huh? Please don't throw out my old PlayStation games." True to form, Will had no complaints or worries other than wondering where she should store some of his video games.

"Oh, you funny boy of mine," said Molly, laughing with relief. "When you get here, you can sort through all your things! Besides we're not moving until the new year!"

Molly had known Will would take the news calmly. That's just who her youngest child had always been—calm and steady. She assumed those were two qualities that the Army most coveted when they recruited EOD specialists. In her heart, Molly had known since Will's earliest years that he had a certain stature—he was serene but physically confident—qualities that had fueled his boyhood dream to enlist in the military. Molly and Bill hoped he would grow out of that stage, and they would then be able to convince him to go to college like all of his friends from high school. They were wrong, for the military was the only topic about which Will, their "easy" child, had ever argued or even fought over with his parents. Throughout Will's high school years, there had been several long, tension filled discussions in which Molly and Bill attempted to persuade their beloved son to attend college before even thinking about joining the military. But Will was determined and insistent, and the night before he enlisted was the only time Molly could ever remember Will being inflexible and unyielding about anything. While Annie and Jenn had always been headstrong, Will never was... except when it came to his firm desire to enlist in the Army. The biggest decision of his young life.

Within weeks of graduating from high school, Will left for Fort McCoy, Wisconsin, for basic training. Ten weeks later, Bill and Molly and the girls attended Will's graduation ceremony, at which time they learned Will had applied for and been accepted into the U.S. Army's Advanced Individual Explosive Ordinance Disposal Training. Molly nearly fainted when Will had proudly announced this at their celebratory dinner at a local restaurant near Fort McCoy. After a long, silent pause, Annie and Jenny began hugging and kissing him, tears streaming down their cheeks. There was no use trying to get Will to change his decision. He'd made his choice, been given his orders and would soon be leaving for thirty-seven weeks of Advanced Training as a specialist whose primary responsibility would be to defuse hidden roadside bombs known as IEDs, improvised explosive devices.

Of course, Will had passed specialist training with flying colors. He came home for a short leave and was then deployed to Afghanistan a few months later. Over the next five years, including three separate deployments to Afghanistan, there wasn't a day that Molly didn't worry about her son. And then this year, just three months ago, the dreaded telephone call came. Will had been injured by a bomb and had been flown to Germany for surgery and recuperation. Now, after several surgeries and three months of recovery at the military hospitals, he was coming home for Christmas! Molly still couldn't believe it.

"Selling the house is a great idea, Mom," said Will after hearing about the house sale. Over the past months, he had been worried about his mother's cancer and whether his dad would be able to help her through the possible ordeal of a long-term illness.

"I just want you to know this doesn't affect Christmas here at all," said Molly. "Like I said, the move will be sometime in the new year."

"Gotcha," said Will. After a moment he asked, "How are you feeling?"

"Oh, I'm fine, Will. Don't worry about me; I look younger in my blonde wig!"

"I'm sure you look great."

"Oh, Will, I just can't wait for you to get here."

"Me, too. And, ah, hey Mom?" Will paused for a moment.

Whenever her son had some kind of proposal to present to her, Molly knew it always started with 'Ah, hey Mom?' So, she gladly offered her standard, unhampered response. "Yes?"

"I invited one of my combat buddies to stay with us for Christmas. I hope that's okay with you and Dad."

Will knew it would be more than okay with his parents. It always had been okay with them ever since he was five years old and would bring home stray children for an afternoon of play and, more often than not, a place that evening at the Taylors' dinner table. Once, to Molly and Bill's utter astonishment, Will had brought home Daryl, the very same boy who had relentlessly bullied their son at school. Though taken aback, they and their girls had warmly welcomed Daryl into their home and had watched as, over time, Daryl and Will developed a remarkable bond of friendship.

"That's wonderful, Will. I'll make sure the guestroom is ready for him."

"I knew you would, Mom. Thanks!"

# CHAPTER 7

JENNY LOVED HER job as an interior decorator with the Riverside Home and Office Design Group. Located in an old warehouse on Main Street in Moonlight Falls, its backside facing the river, the company had begun in 2010 with just two partners. By the time Jenny had received her degree, the company had grown into a leading design and architectural firm and had begun recruiting young, talented designers to join them. Jenny arrived with just the type of skills and talent they were hoping to find. She quickly acquired new clients in and around Moonlight Falls and all the way into the Twin Cities. During her various internships, Jenny had worked on many of the more modern downtown office buildings. But her specialty was in redesigning the interiors of some of the old Tudor and Gothic styled homes along Summit Avenue in St. Paul, of similar vintage and style as some of the old mansions along the St. Croix River near Moonlight Falls, the very homes she had so admired as a young girl. Jenny still held onto her childhood dream of buying and restoring one of those homes, but for now, she and Sam were very content to be living in their beautiful little cottage on River Cove Lane.

Jenny had decided the call with Annie would have to wait

until after her next appointment with the partners at Moonlight Falls Physical Therapy Clinic, just a few minutes' drive to Old Town, at the opposite end of Main Street from her own office. She had not been thrilled when the clinic remodeling pitch was assigned to her, because she assumed, like most new businesses, it would mean working with an inexperienced client with a tiny budget and high expectations; and worse, the client would probably be steering her toward some sort of high-tech, modern design, her least favorite style.

Two hours later, as Jenny left the meeting, she was feeling excited and very impressed with the three young owners of the clinic, each of whom had a medical degree in physical therapy—one specialized in orthopedic therapy, one in sports therapy, and one in pediatric therapy. During the consultation meeting with Jenny, the three therapists made it clear they did not want the clinic's entryway and reception areas to feel formal or inhospitable. They wanted Jenny to turn the current sterile and impersonal entryway into a warm and welcoming environment—a "happy zone," they called it—where their clients, whether they were children or seniors, would immediately feel safe, optimistic and well cared for. Jenny already had several design ideas running through her head as she drove back toward her office on the north edge of town. She looked at her watch and decided she had just enough time to call Annie before her next appointment.

"Hey," Annie answered. "Good timing. Emma and I just got home. Can you talk to Emma for a second while I get her wheelchair out of the car?"

Not waiting for an answer, Annie quickly handed her cell phone to Emma, who was seated in the backseat of their van.

"Say 'hi' Emma. It's Aunt Jenny," said Annie.

"Hi, Aunt Jenny." Emma's voice did not sound cheerful.

"Hey, sweetie. You sound tired. Was it a hard day at therapy?"

"Yes, and we had so much traffic on the way home," huffed Emma. "Are you and Uncle Sam coming over for dinner tonight?"

In the background, Jenny could hear the sound of Emma's wheelchair clicking into position. It tugged at Jenny's heart, knowing that her niece needed to be lifted into the chair and then wheeled up a ramp leading to the front door. Before the accident, Emma had been an active and energetic child, running and skipping everywhere she went with an ever-present little girl whistle. And then, in a horrible fraction of a second, the running and skipping and whistling had stopped.

"No, not tonight, Emmy. I'm off to an appointment right now and your Uncle Sam is still in Chicago."

"Oh, yeah. I forgot," Emma said as her mother lifted her out of the van and into the wheelchair.

"But don't forget we have our girlfriend sleepover coming up. Just you and me," said Jenny, smiling to herself.

After the accident last Christmas, and after Emma was finally out of the hospital and back home with Annie, Jenny had coerced Annie into allowing Emma to have weekly sleepovers at Jenny's house. She did this not just because she loved Emma as if she were her own daughter, but also because she knew Annie needed some alone time.

"Can we watch 'Angry Birds' again and drink ginger ale and eat potato chips?"

"Of course!" Jenny laughed because she knew Emma had said this for Annie's benefit. While Annie did not allow Emma to have chips of any kind or sugary, carbonated soft drinks at home, she would happily pretend to be upset that Aunt Jenny gave those treats to Emma on their sleepovers.

"Well, I've got to go, Aunt Jenny," said Emma from her wheelchair.

"So soon?" asked Jenny, playfully whining.

"Yup. I'm in my chair, and I need both of my hands to push me to the house. My therapist says the more I push myself, the more it will help my arm muscles look like Arnold Schwarzenegger's. Ugh." With that, Emma handed the cell phone back to her mother.

"Hey, Jenny. I can talk now," Annie said as she watched Emma wheel herself up the ramp to the front porch.

"Arnold Schwarzenegger?" Jenny asked.

Annie laughed. "Yeah. Emma isn't exactly on board with looking like a weight lifter," Annie said.

"I don't blame her."

Several times, Jenny had accompanied Annie and Emma to therapy sessions way over in Minneapolis, and she was not impressed with the good Dr. Leonard. Based on her observations, Dr. Leonard was much too serious, and he lacked enthusiasm and empathy. Jenny believed Emma needed someone more energetic, someone more kid-friendly and encouraging. More than once she had tried to convince her sister to research and interview other therapists, but Annie was stubborn, insisting Dr. Leonard was the best in the field and that he was exactly the therapist Emma needed to have. Period.

As Jenny pulled into the small parking lot near her office, she continued speaking through the Bluetooth connection. "Annie, listen. I called because Mom told me about selling their house," said Jenny, broaching a subject she knew Annie would want to discuss with her.

"Oh, Jenny, I'm sorry. I know how much you love the house." Annie's voice was filled with concern and compassion. "Did you beg her not to sell?"

"You know me," Jenny conceded. "Actually, I started to have a fit, but then it suddenly occurred to me that maybe Mom and Dad aren't telling us everything, you know, about Mom's cancer.

Maybe they're thinking they need to move to a home without so many stairs, just in case."

"Just in case what, Jenny?"

"I don't know. You see how much weight Mom has lost and how hard it is for her to walk upstairs. Maybe they're preparing for any kind of unforeseen physical challenge." Jenny immediately wished she hadn't used those words. Annie knew better than anyone that there is no way to be prepared for the unexpected in life, no way to be prepared for any number of future unforeseen challenges.

It took Annie a moment to respond to Jenny's inadvertent remark. "You might be right," said Annie.

There was another sad pause, then Jenny broke the silence. "It's just so hard to imagine that this will be our last Christmas in the home where we grew up and had so many wonderful memories. Now, more than ever, I wish…" Jenny's voice trailed off.

Annie could sense Jenny was leading up to something, and so she waited, intuitively knowing what Jenny was about to say.

"Annie, it's just… well, if you and Emma go to Orlando—" Jenny struggled to find the right words. "If you and Emma go to Orlando for Christmas and this is the last one we ever have in our family home, then Emma's only memory of Christmas at home will be last year's." The words stung Annie, but Jenny continued. "That just shouldn't be."

Annie cringed at the sound of her sister's words even though each one was spoken with love and compassion. "I told Mom I would think about it," said Annie, her voice sounding dull and emotionless.

"Have you told Emma, yet? About Mom and Dad moving and—"

"No."

"Annie, please just talk to Emma. Make sure she wouldn't

prefer to be with all of us on Christmas Eve. Maybe, just maybe, it would be good for all of us to help wipe away—"

"Nothing is ever going to wipe away last Christmas Eve, Jenny!"

"I know. But Annie, what if Mom isn't here next—"

"Stop! Stop!" Annie said forcefully. "I can't go there—I *won't* go there!"

Jenny knew she needed to change the subject before her sister hung up on her. "Okay. You're right. Ah, listen, um, I met with a new client today. Interestingly enough, it's a brand-new physical therapy clinic right here in Moonlight Falls. They took over the old Dockside Athletic Club. I'm going to renovate their reception room which is pretty large."

"Nice."

"Yeah, and... I thought I'd tell you about it because I think you might want to look into it... for Emma. There's a very impressive physical therapist who works with kids, and there's also a sports therapist and an orthopedic therapist. I met all three of them—they're the owners and these guys are really impressive. They've got a lot of experience and—"

"Jenn, Emma already has a therapist," interrupted Annie. "The best I could find. I'm not going to have her go to someone new. And besides, you haven't even started to work on the renovation yet, so they aren't even open for patients."

"Oh, no, no, no. They're all moved in, and they're using the old gym as a therapy area. You should see all the equipment and machines they've got. I'm just working on the entryway and the reception areas. They want me to make the place feel warmer and more inviting."

For just a second, Annie thought of the dreary clinic at the university where she took Emma three times a week. "Ah. Well,

I'm still not going to change Emma's therapist," said Annie. As Jenny knew, Annie could be more headstrong than anyone.

"Listen, I know you're going to hate me for this, and you may never speak to me again, but I made an appointment for you and Emma to see Dr. Christopher, one of the therapists."

"What?!"

"It's for tomorrow morning at ten-thirty. I know Emma doesn't have therapy tomorrow so—"

"Soooo, we have other things to do, Jenny!"

"Just listen to me for a second." Annie was very familiar with her sister's stubborn streak. "This clinic's a five-minute drive from your house. Think of that as you sit in traffic three times a week, ninety minutes each way."

Annie was simultaneously angry at her sister and attracted to the idea of Emma not having to spend several hours each week in the car, especially in the winter.

"And who knows, maybe this therapist is really good. And maybe Emma will like him better than grumpy old Dr. Leonard over at the U."

Annie did not need to be reminded that Emma was not in love with Dr. Leonard's formal and impersonal approach. The man had never once cracked a smile or tried to make a human connection with Emma.

"Okay, Jenn. Emma and I will go see this Dr. Christopher tomorrow, but only because I know you won't leave me alone unless we go. But I want you to understand that a shorter drive is not going to make me change Emma's therapy program."

"I understand," said Jenny, knowing her sales skills had risen to the occasion and that she had just closed the deal. "Let me know how it goes."

In truth, the main reason Annie agreed to her sister's request was because Annie had been worried about Jenny for some time. It was no secret that Jenny and Sam had tried several times over the past years to become pregnant. After too many miscarriages, the most recent one just five months ago, Jenny had told Annie that she'd given up on the idea of having a child. She had seemed to be coping well enough, but Annie could tell that her sister was overcompensating for the miscarriages by adding to her already heavy workload. Jenny's expertise was in restoring older homes and buildings, and a year ago she would never have considered taking on designing a measly reception area for a small physical therapy clinic in a 1920s-era gym. But then, a year ago, before Molly was diagnosed with breast cancer, their parents would never have considered selling their home. A year ago, before the accident, Annie would never have dreamed she'd be working from home part-time for Flatiron Sports in order to home school Emma and oversee her physical therapy. And a year ago, Will had not been injured in Afghanistan, and the thought of retiring from the Army had never crossed his mind.

PART THREE

# REHABILITATION

# CHAPTER 8

AT 10:30 SHARP the next morning, Annie pulled into the parking lot of a place she had known all her life—the Dockside Men's Club, an aging brick and wood three-story building that dated back to the 1920s. While she had no memory of ever having been inside—it was, after all, For Men Only as far back as she could remember—she had driven past the building hundreds of times and had always thought it looked a little creepy. Annie parked her van and took note of the large, newly installed, double front doors and the fresh coat of a tasteful wintergreen paint on the eaves and shutters. Mounted and centered above the glass front doors was a large sign announcing the new occupants: **Moonlight Falls Physical Therapy Clinic.**

After lifting Emma into her wheelchair, Annie wheeled her daughter across the parking lot and up the ramp that led to the front doors. In moments, they had entered a large, dark room in which Annie saw a timeworn reception desk and a young girl, twenty years old at most, sitting behind the desk, reading a novel. Her eyes brightened at the site of two visitors.

"Good morning," said the receptionist. She could easily have passed for an eighth grader.

"Hi. I'm Emma, and I'm here to meet Dr. Christopher," said Emma.

The young girl smiled at Emma and spoke directly to her. "Dr. Chris is looking forward to meeting you, Emma. He's running just a little bit late, but he asked me to give you something while you waited." The receptionist stood up and walked away from her desk and toward Emma. She was obviously hiding something behind her back.

Emma looked intrigued as the smiling receptionist bent down to Emma's level and placed a soft, cuddly teddy bear on Emma's lap.

"Ohhhh," Emma whispered as she wrapped her arms around the soft teddy. "She's beautiful."

Annie silently groaned to herself, knowing the gift was an obvious marketing tool designed to sell Emma on the clinic. What child wouldn't love a teddy bear with the words Moonlight Falls PT Clinic embroidered along the edges of the kerchief tied around its neck? This definitely placed Annie on the defensive, knowing she would have to tell Emma that this was *not* where she would be having her physical therapy. Annie noticed some business cards on the reception counter. She picked up one and saw the full name: Nicholas A. Christopher, M.D. Physical, Kinesiological and Cardiovascular Therapy.

Emma held the teddy bear, cuddling it to her chest as if she would never let go. "What's his name?" Emma asked the receptionist.

"Hmm," said the receptionist, tilting her head. "That's a good question, Emma. I don't know his name yet because *you* need to give him his name. But I can tell you my name. I'm Lisa."

"Thank you, Lisa," Emma stretched her arms to give the receptionist a hug.

Annie looked around the reception area. It was a large room

with ancient, cracking pine walls painted institutional grey, faded in many areas where the old wood was pushing through. Despite its size, the whole room felt suffocating. A collection of tacky, powder-blue plastic chairs lined the perimeter, looking like leftovers from an abandoned church basement. The floor was a mixture of warped oak slats and peeling green linoleum, and the most prominent features on the walls were framed copies of various magazine covers from the 1950s. Someone's idea of decorations, Annie surmised. She could see why the clinic had hired Jenny to make some changes. Redesigning this space would definitely be a challenge.

A tall, dark haired, thirty-something man walked into the room. He had noticed the dismayed and condemning look on Annie's face as she sized up the surroundings. "Kind of depressing, isn't it?" said the man.

Annie noticed a name tag pinned to his shirt: *Dr. Christopher.* Despite being startled and downright mortified that her negative assessment had been so obvious, Annie was candid in her response. "In a word… yes." Annie smiled and shrugged her shoulders with embarrassment over her disapproving first impression.

The man laughed out loud. "I hate it, too, but with your sister's help, we're in the midst of redesigning this entire space. It can't happen soon enough." He then walked over to Emma and reached out to shake her hand. "Hi there, I'm Dr. Chris. And who are you?" The doctor's voice was cheerful, not patronizing, and his smile was genuinely warm.

Emma extended her hand. "I'm Emma, and I don't want to look like Arnold Schwarzenegger."

Once again, the young doctor laughed out loud. "I don't blame you. I don't want to look like him either."

Emma smiled at Dr. Chris.

"So, if you don't want to look like a great big bodybuilder, what do you want to look like?" Dr. Chris asked earnestly.

"I want to look like me when I could walk. I want you to teach my legs to walk again."

Annie was stunned by Emma's blunt, honest words compared to how tentative and withdrawn she had always been with Dr. Leonard.

Dr. Chris looked kindly into Emma's eyes. "Emma, I can't promise you that I will be able to teach your legs to walk," he said in a gentle but forthright manner. "But I do promise you, and your mom, that I will use everything I have learned as a doctor and everything in my power, to help your legs learn how to walk again."

Emma nodded and gazed into the doctor's eyes as if awestruck.

"But you have to promise me that you will do everything within your power to help your legs walk. That means lots of hard work here at the clinic and lots of hard work at home."

Emma's eyes had remained locked onto the doctor's eyes as if she were analyzing every word Dr. Chris was saying. And then, she took his right hand in hers. "Deal!" she said loudly, vigorously shaking his hand. Dr. Chris and Emma continued shaking hands as if a contract had been signed, sealed and delivered and no other party, like her mom, for instance, need be involved.

"Deal!" the doctor answered. He looked up at Annie, whose eyes and facial expression were putting the kibosh on any sort of deal. "But first things first. I'd like you and your mom to come with me into the therapy gym and meet our other therapists."

Dr. Chris stood up, turned towards Annie and reached out to shake her hand.

"I'm Dr. Christopher. And you're Annie. Your sister is very fond of you."

Annie accepted Dr. Christopher's hand but was unprepared for the firm warmth of his handshake.

He then reached for the handles on the back of Emma's wheelchair and asked, "May I?"

"Of course," said Annie, following Dr. Chris as he pushed Emma's wheelchair through the reception area and into a bright gymnasium filled with medicine balls, ropes, tables and various computer stations and other high-tech physical therapy equipment. Annie was astounded by the size of the gym and the vast array of gear.

"I know. It's pretty darn big, isn't it?" He was reading Annie's mind.

"Wow!" Emma said as she turned her head in every direction to take in all that the place had to offer.

There were other patients in the room, some doing various exercises and therapies under the direction of therapists who wore identical khaki slacks and green polo shirts with "Moonlight Falls PT Clinic" embroidered on their front pockets.

"That's Dr. Joni over there," said Dr. Chris, waving at a short, dark-haired woman in her late twenties.

"Hi everyone," said Dr. Joni, returning the wave.

"And that's Dr. Tom, the muscleman over by the weights," added Dr. Chris. He was right about the muscles—Dr. Tom was an African American who looked like he might have been a professional football player. "He's a specialist in sports medicine and, yes, he played some football himself—for a team called the Vikings."

Annie nodded, impressed, certain that Ron would have recognized the man's name.

"Howdy, yawl," said Dr. Tom with a bright Texas drawl. "Welcome!" He was spotting a young man on a trampoline who looked like he might be a gymnast.

Emma pointed to another client with braces on the calves of his legs who was pushing on the exercise bike pedals. "Can I ride that bike someday?"

"Anything is possible," said Dr. Chris with a smile. He could tell by the look on Annie's face that she was not supportive of any kind of bicycle workout or any kind of therapy at this clinic. "You won't believe it, Emma, but through those doors," he said, pointing across the gym's hardwood floor, "there's an Olympic-sized swimming pool where we do a lot of swim therapy."

"Really? I used to swim all the time. Can I see the pool?" Unlike her mother, Emma had no reservations about this clinic.

"Sure," said Dr. Chris, bending down to Emma's level. "But first, can you show me how well you can wheel yourself around the room?"

Emma's eyes lit up. She started pushing her chair around the gym in a zig-zag pattern.

Dr. Chris and Annie watched Emma, and then, almost involuntarily, their eyes met, and they smiled at each other. Annie felt her face begin to blush and had to quickly look away in order to give one hundred percent of her attention to Emma, who was confidently maneuvering her wheelchair between several large floor mats. Emma was definitely trying to impress the doctor with the muscle strength she had developed in her arms.

"Dr. Christopher," Annie began as she walked beside the doctor toward the doors leading to the swimming pool.

"It's Dr. Chris to everyone here," said the young man, trying to put Annie at ease with his informality. "Kind of charming, don't you think?"

Annie couldn't help but grin when Dr. Chris winked at her. "Ahhh, right, very charming," she smirked with more than a little sarcasm.

"As you may know, this building was once called Dockside Athletic Club."

"I *do* know. I grew up in Moonlight Falls."

"So, did your family have a membership?"

"Oh, no," said Annie cynically. "The club was open to men only, and my dad had no interest in joining a club that my mom and his daughters couldn't join. Besides, the place had a bit of a reputation," she said, pausing for dramatic effect. "It was, you know, exclusively for wealthy old men, and so it became known as the Dockside Cocktail Club."

"So, I've heard," said Dr. Chris.

"I'm guessing the bar got more use than the gym," Annie said with a bit of a grin.

"Did they ever allow women to become members?"

"Nope, they stuck to their ways until the membership dwindled down to a few old men with canes. Times changed, and some smaller, less expensive athletic clubs popped up in town, and the idea of a stuffy old men's club just faded away."

"I guess it's time had come and gone," added Dr. Chris.

"The building has been vacant for a long time… in fact, a lot of townspeople have been worried that the building would deteriorate and become an eyesore," said Annie. "I'm sure everyone in town is breathing a sigh of relief now that your clinic has taken over."

Dr. Chris looked around the two-tiered gymnasium. "It's a little bigger than what my partners and I had in mind when we went looking for a space to begin our practice, but I think we'll grow into it. With the pool and the gym, it really fit our needs."

Emma rolled her chair beside Dr. Chris.

"Follow me," said Dr. Chris as the electronic double-paned doors opened to reveal a stunning, crystal blue, Olympic-sized swimming pool. A whiff of chlorine immediately filled Annie's senses. A lone swimmer holding onto a paddleboard slowly kicked his way along one of the lanes.

"That's what I want to do," said Emma, pointing at the swimmer.

"Well, then we've got some work to do," said Dr. Chris as he wheeled Emma around the edge of the pool.

"My daddy and I used to swim at Pike's Lake all the time in the summer when the water was warm. We belonged to the Swim Club."

Emma looked at her mother with longing in her eyes. "I was really fast, wasn't I Mommy?"

"Yes, you were." Annie smiled and nodded even though her heart was breaking. Annie looked at Dr. Chris. "She was like a fish, starting when she was about three. You can't grow up around here without learning how to swim," said Annie.

"I bet," said Dr. Chris, escorting Annie and Emma out of the pool area and into his nearby office where he gestured for Annie to sit down on a guest chair.

Annie had come prepared with a notebook filled with written reports, x-rays of Emma's spinal and leg injuries, notes regarding the kind of therapy she'd already had, along with evaluations made by Dr. Leonard at the university.

Dr. Chris scanned the pages while Emma and Annie sat in silence. Finally, he looked up and said, "You know, I trained under Dr. Leonard."

"Oh, really?" Annie was surprised and impressed by this news, although it didn't matter, because Annie was not going to change Emma's therapists. "Dr. Leonard has an incredible reputation."

"He's the best," added Dr. Chris.

Emma didn't look thrilled by this revelation. In fact, she frowned in dismay. To Emma, Dr. Leonard had always seemed stern and humorless. This Dr. Chris was not like that at all. He was younger and smiled more. Emma worried that when Dr. Chris said Dr. Leonard was the best, he was also implying she should stay with grumpy old Dr. Leonard.

"Not only is he one of the nation's most respected physical therapists, but he's considered to be the best of the best when it comes to spinal cord injuries," added Dr. Chris. "Everything I've learned about this kind of therapy comes from my studies under Dr. Leonard."

Emma slumped her shoulder and bent her head. She had already made up her mind that she wanted to change therapists. *Didn't she and Dr. Chris have a deal? Had he forgotten about their handshake?*

Dr. Chris spoke directly to Emma. "So, if you and your mom decide to come here for your therapy, I would want to keep in contact with Dr. Leonard to pick up where he left off and get his advice about what we need to do next."

Emma looked at Dr. Chris and smiled. "That's okay with me," she said, quickly looking at her mother, her eyes begging for Annie to agree.

"Emma, we need to talk with Dr. Leonard before we make any decisions." Annie saw the look of desperation Emma's eyes. "But it would be nice if we didn't have to drive all the way into the city three times a week."

# CHAPTER 9

WHEN NICHOLAS CHRISTOPHER was four, he dreamed of becoming a trash collector. He wanted to operate the big, green trash trucks that passed slowly by his house in Montclair, New Jersey, on garbage day, making wonderful loud, crashing, hydraulic-lifting noises as large trash bins were emptied into its inner chamber. But by the time Nick turned seven, he had a much bigger dream—that of becoming a ninja warrior and saving the world from evil forces. He was pretty certain that was what he would become when he was all grown up; that is, until around age ten when trash collectors and ninja warriors faded away to make room for his dream of becoming a professional soccer player. Morning until night, Nick lived and breathed soccer, so the sad thing about this dream was that it didn't just fade away like the others. It was obliterated forever on the day his sister Lizzie fell from a swing in their backyard and broke her neck.

Nick was thirteen and Lizzie had just turned five when she was brought home from the hospital to spend the rest of her days in bed, needing and receiving around-the-clock care. Whenever the therapist came to work on stretching and massaging Lizzie's legs and arms, Nick would stand by her side and ask the therapist to teach him the same techniques so when the therapist wasn't there, Nick could take over and perform the same exercises several times a day. He no longer played soccer or participated in other after school programs; his focus was on schoolwork and Lizzie. Nick devoted most of his free time to entertaining her and giving her the prescribed exercises and stretching movements, relentlessly determined that Lizzie's arms and legs would not atrophy. Despite all of his efforts, and his neverending hope that Lizzie would walk again, Lizzie died three years later. Then sixteen years old, Nick knew he would devote the rest of his life to helping people with spinal cord injuries like his sister's. His undergraduate studies in biology at Northwestern University led him to being accepted to the Department of Physical Therapy (DPT) program at the University of Minnesota Medical School.

Around the time Nick was about to complete his residency, he had become engaged to a woman who had gone through the rigors of medical school with him. They had been together for nearly four years and thought they were in love with each other, but by the time they had reached graduation they had both realized something was missing in their relationship. So, she moved to back to Chicago to be closer to her family, and even though Nick had grown up in suburban New York City, and his parents still lived there, he had decided to remain in Minneapolis. Uncertain where he would ultimately land, Nick began working part-time doing physical therapy for the Minnesota Vikings football team.

A chance meeting with Dr. Jerry Arnold at a Minnesota Viking "Stadium Club" luncheon a year later led to a rare opportunity. The retired Dr. Arnold, who dabbled in real estate in and around Moonlight Falls, had purchased the Dockside Athletic Club for a song years earlier in hopes of turning it into a hotel. But when he met the young and ambitious Dr. Nicholas Christopher, he instead offered to finance a private, state-of-the-art physical therapy clinic in the old building. Dr. Arnold was so impressed with Nick and his two partners that he backed the funding for the necessary renovations and the latest, most current therapy equipment and technology available to help the physically handicapped. It had taken eight months to complete the remodeling and install the new gear. Meanwhile, architectural plans were also created for renovating the two upper floors of the building, where once there had been small apartments for out-of-town guests of the Athletic Club's members. Now, the plans to convert those guest apartments into short-term suites were on hold while they finished up the final renovations of the first-floor therapy areas.

By the time Jenny had met the partners of the Moonlight Falls PT Clinic, the clinic had been operating for a little over two months, even though certain areas of the facility still needed updating, including the reception area. At the conclusion of Jenny's interview, during which she had offered off-the-cuff ideas for the interior design, she was hired on the spot. Jenny had been particularly impressed with Dr. Christopher, who had escorted her to the parking lot.

"We'd like you to get started immediately," Dr. Christopher had said as he walked alongside Jenny.

Jenny promised she would follow up with a written agreement, and then, just before getting into her car, she asked the doctor if he would be willing to meet with her niece. "Her name's Emma," said Jenny. "She's six years old and was in a terrible accident last Christmas. It left her in a wheelchair due to a spinal cord injury."

That first morning when Emma arrived at the clinic, Dr. Chris was prepared to meet with Emma and her mother, but he wasn't prepared for the shock of how much Emma reminded him of his sister, Lizzie. His heart jumped the instant she shook his hand and told him she didn't want to look like Arnold Schwarzenegger, but she did want her legs to walk again. How many times had his sister said the same thing? *I want my legs to walk again* had become Lizzie's mantra before she died, so when Emma uttered those exact words with the same determination of his sister, Dr. Chris felt his heartbreak all over again.

Without warning, Nick was instantly drawn to Emma and wanted nothing more than to help her as much as he could. In the brief hour that he spent with her and her mother, showing them around the building, he had become so emotionally attached to Emma that he almost slipped up and called her Lizzie. He explained the innovative kinds of therapies they were using, supported by recent clinical studies that focused on improving brain-to-muscle movement in people with spinal cord injuries. While the information was way above Emma's capacity to under-stand, she seemed excited by everything she heard and saw, unlike her mother who seemed reticent and skeptical about the clinic and even about Dr. Chris.

By the time Emma and Annie had left the clinic, Dr. Chris knew Emma was ready to start working with him immediately, but he wasn't so sure he had convinced Annie Morgan.

After their meeting with Dr. Christopher, Annie drove home through the Meadows, past the home where she grew up, taking the long way back toward Pike's Lake, avoiding the steep hill that had claimed her husband's life. From the date of the tragedy until now, she had not driven up or down what was locally called Nor-wegian Hill. Not once. Driving through her old neighborhood, Annie was a little confused about Moonlight Falls PT Clinic and this new therapist, Dr. Christopher, although she knew very well how Emma felt. Annie firmly believed she had already found the best therapist for Emma—Dr. Leonard. But during their visit, Dr. Christopher had told her about the possibility of using FES, *functional electrical stimulation,* for Emma. Annie knew what FES was, having researched it months ago. However, Dr. Leonard dismissed its use because it was still in the early research stages, and there were questions about its use on younger patients. "Not enough empirical data is available," was the way she remembered Dr. Leonard responding to her inquiry. So, on Dr. Leonard's advice, Annie had shelved the idea.

Once home, Annie waited until Emma was napping before calling Dr. Leonard and seeking his advice. It came as no surprise that Dr. Leonard thought very highly of Dr. Christopher and his partners, but she *was* surprised when he actually recommended moving Emma's therapy to the Moonlight Falls Clinic. He mentioned that Dr. Christopher had already contacted him about Emma, which impressed Annie, and he informed her that Dr. Christopher and he would, in effect, collaborate on things like strategy, data gathering and performance goals for Emma.

A few days later Emma began a five-days-a-week therapy program at Moonlight Falls PT Clinic. With Dr. Chris.

Annie marveled at how Emma's attitude toward therapy had changed overnight. Before starting therapy with Dr. Chris, Annie would have to bribe and beg Emma to work on her exercises; now, Emma was initiating the practice times at home. Annie was also stunned, yet so very grateful, at how motivated Emma was during her therapy sessions with Dr. Chris. He was encouraging and patient, making sure to explain to Emma the purpose of each exercise. And he often slipped in a silly story or joke between exercises, which Emma would excitedly repeat to Annie that night at home.

# CHAPTER 10

ONE LATE AFTERNOON in early December, at the end of Emma's first week with Dr. Chris, Annie sat on a floor mat in the Moonlight Falls Clinic, thinking about Emma's therapy progress. Dr. Chris had asked her to watch closely as he slowly rotated Emma's feet, one by one, first to the right and then to the left. Dr. Leonard had used the same technique on Emma, but he'd never had Emma wear a vest that that triggered tiny electric shocks up and down her spinal column. The good news was that Emma could feel some of the electric shocks in her lower back. The bad news was that Emma felt nothing below her pelvis, even as Dr. Chris had continued to rotate Emma's feet from the ankle down.

"So, you're going to take the vest home with you, and you have to do these exercises six times a day. Every day," said Dr. Chris, handing her the vest. "And if you want to do them even more times a day, that would be amazing."

"Aye, aye, Captain Chris!" Emma giggled and saluted her doctor. In a short time, Emma and Dr. Chris had established a bond with each other that both pleased and mystified Annie.

"Okay! And I don't want to hear from your mom that there is

any complaining about how hard it is to do all the exercises." Dr. Chris winked at Annie as he gave the order.

Annie smiled and felt her face flush.

"Well… since you're my last appointment of the day, let me lock up the place, and I'll escort you both to the parking lot."

"Oh, that's not really necessary," said Annie, firmly. She was both puzzled by the offer and puzzled as to why she felt uncomfortable leaving the clinic with Dr. Chris. It was five o'clock, the end of the day, so it would be very dark outside and probably still snowing as it had been when they had arrived two hours earlier. If the older Dr. Leonard had made the same offer, Annie would have been grateful. But for the moment, for reasons she could not explain, Annie felt uneasy and awkward having Dr. Chris walk out the door with them.

"That's great, Dr. Chris!" Emma said. "Maybe you could help my mom put the wheelchair in the car. It's kind of hard for her."

"Emma!?" Annie was surprised and embarrassed that her daughter was doing her bidding.

"She grunts a whole lot when she lifts it into the trunk," said Emma with a cute little giggle.

Annie glared at her daughter, giving her the stink-eye.

Dr. Christopher laughed. "Wait for me by the front door," he said as he walked to the far corner of the gym.

Lights began shutting down one at a time until only a few lights in the reception room were still glowing. Annie looked out the reception window, and when she saw that the snow had stopped, she pushed Emma's wheelchair through the automatic doors and toward the handicapped parking space where her van was parked. Even though Emma had needed a wheelchair for almost a year, it still felt odd to Annie to park in designated handicapped spots. They were for older people, not for her six-year-old daughter.

"Mommy, aren't you going to wait for Dr. Chris?"

"We don't need his help, sweetie. Look, it stopped snowing."

Annie opened the sliding door of the van and lifted Emma into her seat, then quickly collapsed the wheelchair. As she heaved the wheelchair into the back of the van, Annie wondered if she were in denial by not buying a van that was equipped with a special hydraulic wheelchair lift, as her mother had suggested. Emma was light and the wheelchair wasn't too awkward; besides, she still held out hope that one day Emma would walk again—that there would be no wheelchair and no need to park in any handicap zone.

Annie walked to the front of the van and opened the door.

"It's cold, Mommy."

"Once I start the car, I'll get the heater going."

Annie pushed the starter button and was dismayed to hear a grinding sound coming from under the hood. She pushed the button again, and there was no grinding sound this time, just a "click-click." And then no sound at all. A yellow light appeared on the dashboard with the word Service. There was also an image of an oil gage blinking on and off.

"Ohhhhhhhhh," Annie moaned and lightly thumped her forehead against the steering wheel as she tried to remember how long she had ignored the light that had been warning her to get the car serviced.

A tapping sound at the window caused Annie to look up and see Dr. Chris motioning for her to wind down her window. Despite feeling completely embarrassed that he'd seen her hitting her head on the steering wheel, she pushed the window button. She waited a second and then realized that, of course, the window would not go down because the engine was dead. Or worse. Sheepishly, Annie opened the door.

"That doesn't sound too good," he said.

"Nope."

Dr. Chris looked up at the sky. A light snow was beginning to fall again.

"Let me call for a tow truck, and then I'll drive you and Emma back to your place."

Annie didn't see any other choice, so she and Emma waited inside Dr. Chris's car with the heater on until the tow truck arrived. After signing off with the driver, Dr. Chris hopped into the driver's seat of his car and rubbed his hands.

"Thanks so much for calling them," said Annie.

"Not a problem," said Dr. Chris. He turned around and looked at Emma, who had a big smile on her face.

# CHAPTER 11

EMMA WAS ANIMATED the entire way home, chatting with Dr. Chris as if he were her very best friend. "Do you know what tonight is?" Emma asked Dr. Chris as he drove up their driveway and parked the car.

Dr. Chris pushed a button on his dashboard, shutting off his car engine, then turned to look at Emma in the backseat. "No, I don't Emma. What night is tonight?"

"Pizza night! Every Friday is pizza night!" Emma laughed.

"That's just about the best kind of night there is," said Dr. Chris, laughing. He opened his door and walked to the trunk to retrieve Emma's wheelchair. As he did this, Annie walked to the backseat door and carefully lifted Emma out of the car and into her arms.

Dr. Chris assembled the wheelchair and pushed it over to them.

"What kind of pizza do you like?" Emma asked Dr. Chris as Annie carefully placed her on the seat of the chair.

Annie looked at her daughter, knowing from experience that she was on her way to becoming one of the all-time great connivers.

"Mm, that's a hard one, because I like just about every kind there is, but I would have to say that my favorite kind of pizza is cheese only," responded Dr. Chris, remembering that "cheese only" had been his sister's favorite.

As Dr. Chris pushed the wheelchair along the brick pathway leading to the front porch, he noticed that while most of the houses on the street were colorfully decorated with strings of twinkly lights, Annie's and Emma's house looked dark and cheerless, devoid of anything resembling Christmas.

"That's my favorite, too!" Emma squealed happily. "Do you want to have pizza with us tonight?"

"Oh, Emma. Dr. Chris needs to get home to his family." Annie was mortified that Emma had invited him. She once again gave her daughter a reproachful look.

"I'm really, really hungry and there's no one at my house fixing dinner." Dr. Chris looked at Annie and for the second time that day he winked at her. "So, if your mom says it's okay, I'd love to share some of your cheese pizza tonight."

*What was with the winking?* Annie wondered. It had once again caused her to blush and feel vulnerable. And it had stirred up a feeling inside her that she hadn't felt in a very long time.

"Well," said Annie with a quixotic sigh, "I guess we'll need to order a large pizza tonight." She smiled awkwardly at the doctor, then unlocked the front door and turned on the lights in the living room.

"Extra-large, Mommy!"

Dr. Chris pushed Emma into the house and noticed there was no Christmas tree; in fact, there were no Christmas decorations anywhere to be seen.

"I'll call for the pizza," said Annie. She walked into the dining room and turned on the lights, then walked into the kitchen to look for the pizza parlor's phone number.

"I see you two haven't gotten a Christmas tree yet." Dr. Chris looked at Emma, who seemed a little embarrassed by his observation.

"We aren't going to get one this year," she said. "And we're not even going to have lights outside. I wish we had at least put some lights on the front porch and on the fence, but my mom said 'no,' and no means no."

Dr. Chris laughed quietly to himself as Annie entered the room, having overheard her daughter's explanation. "Did you tell Dr. Chris what we're doing instead?"

"Mommy and I are going to Orlando for Christmas." Emma looked up at her mother and smiled.

"Whoa! That sounds like a very cool place to spend Christmas!" said Dr. Chris, looking both sincere and excited.

"I guess," said Emma, looking away from him as if she wasn't so sure. Then she added, "Except my grandma and grandpa, and my Aunt Jenny and Uncle Sam will still be here, and my Uncle Will is going to be here, too. He's in the United States Army, and he was wounded. But he's going to be okay."

Dr. Chris quickly looked at Annie, who nodded her head reassuringly.

"I'm glad he's going to be okay," said Dr. Chris.

"Emma's never been to Disney World," said Annie, quickly changing the subject to avoid talking about Christmas.

"I've never been there either, so you'll have to tell me all about it when you get back," said Dr. Chris as he looked out the window. "Wow. Come here, Emma. It's snowing very hard outside."

Emma wheeled over to the large picture window and pointed to a fir tree in the middle of the front yard. "Daddy planted that tree the day I was born, and every Christmas he and I put lots and lots of twinkly lights all around it."

"I can tell that's a very special tree, Emma." Dr. Chris thought of the first Christmas after his sister had died, and he knew the depth of loss Emma must have been feeling.

"Emmy, the pizza should be here any minute," said Annie. "Why don't you go wash up, and then we'll be all ready to eat when it arrives."

"Okay," said Emma. She wheeled herself out of the living room and down the hallway leading to the bathroom where a sink had been customized for her.

With Emma out of the room, Annie looked at Dr. Chris as if to say *see why we can't stay here for Christmas*. "I don't know if I'm doing the right thing for Emma," said Annie.

"I can't imagine how difficult this Christmas must be for you both."

"I keep wondering if I'm doing it more for myself than for Emma," said Annie, her eyes suddenly and uncontrollably watering. "It's just that our memories of last year are so painful."

Dr. Chris gently put his hand on Annie's shoulder. "You're doing the right thing by having a different kind of holiday."

Annie felt grateful for the doctor's words of understanding and, oddly, the touch of his hand felt comforting. The doorbell rang.

"Let me get this." Dr. Chris walked to the door to pay the pizza delivery man.

Emma rolled herself into the dining room and watched as her mom placed paper napkins and paper plates on the table. "I have a great idea," Emma announced, "Let's play Old Maid while we eat!"

"Old Maid? I love Old Maid," Dr. Chris said as he entered the dining room carrying an extra-large pizza box. He placed it on the table and sat down across from Emma.

"I have to warn you, Dr. Chris. Emma is pretty sneaky at cards," said Annie from the kitchen. "And she's hard to beat."

Annie carried a tray into the dining room with three cups of hot chocolate, each topped with marshmallows. She placed the cups in front of each of their plates, then sat down next to Emma who was already holding the deck of Old Maid cards.

"This is the best pizza night ever," said the young girl from her wheelchair. "Should I deal first?"

Four hours later Annie stood in the doorway of Emma's bedroom and gazed at her daughter asleep in her bed, so peaceful. With no explanation, a lump formed in Annie's throat, and her eyes began to well up with tears. Emma had been so happy playing cards and chatting with Dr. Chris throughout the night. Annie remembered how she'd been on edge when Dr. Chris had accepted Emma's invitation to stay for pizza. But now, standing in Emma's doorway with tears slowly running down her cheeks, she realized that by the time she had eaten her first slice of pizza she was no longer on edge.

In fact, she had been very happy as she watched the natural interaction and cute interplay between her daughter and Dr. Chris. Looking back on the evening, Annie was surprised that she had not protested more forcefully when Emma had asked Dr. Chris to read her a goodnight story in bed. And after Emma was asleep and Dr. Chris joined Annie in the kitchen, it had seemed only natural to offer him a cup of tea before he left.

They had sat together at the kitchen table for another hour talking about Moonlight Falls and about Dr. Chris's educational background and Annie's educational background and everything else that kept them from getting too personal until Dr. Chris told Annie about his sister's backyard accident and her ultimate death. He had been so open about the pain and loss he had felt over several years, and still felt, and then ever so gently the conversation had turned to Annie's loss of a loving husband and Emma's loss of an adoring father. Annie shared with Dr. Chris the initial shock and pain and the struggle to make life good again for Emma.

It confused Annie that she'd felt comfortable sharing these things with Dr. Chris when she refused to share the intensity of these feelings with anyone else, not even with her mom and dad, nor with her sister or brother. And then she began to feel guilty, since Ron had been the only person she had ever shared such personal feelings with.

Still standing in the doorway, she let her mind slowly, softly fill with memories of happy nights with Ron and Emma. She could almost feel Ron's presence standing beside her, his arm around her shoulders, looking in at their beautiful daughter who was peacefully, happily and soundly asleep.

Annie wiped away the stream of tears and wondered if the pain would ever go away. *Did she even want it to go away?* For Annie, holding onto the pain meant holding onto Ron.

# CHAPTER 12

DRIVING AWAY FROM Annie Morgan's home, Dr. Nicholas Christopher was deep in thought about the evening he had just spent with Annie and Emma. He liked driving along the winding roads in the Pikes Woods area, and with the gentle snow piling up on the streets and his desire to relive every detail about the evening, he drove slowly, listening to a Kenny G holiday album, losing himself momentarily in the beautiful music. At the same time, he was grappling with an odd mixture of emotions—some disquieting, others rather pleasant.

Years ago, he'd played Old Maid countless times with his little sister Lizzie and, like Emma, Old Maid had been her favorite game. A wave of melancholy swept over Nick as he remembered the very last time Lizzie and he had played Old Maid together. She had begged him to play one more hand of the card game. But Nick, being a thirteen-year-old, had had enough and refused. When Lizzie angrily threw the cards at him and called him 'stupid-head' he had laughed at her and left the room.

An hour later, Lizzie had fallen from the swing in their back-yard.

If only he could have gone back in time... *if only*, the two worst words in the English language. But over time, Nick had made peace with himself, knowing that *if only* thoughts cannot and do not change things. Nick shook his head to dull the memory.

The car's windshield wipers slowly pushed away the falling snow, allowing Nick to see the many houses in the area that glowed with the warmth of Christmas lights, and he thought about Annie and Emma's house, which may not have been glowing on the outside, but it glowed on the inside with the warmth and love Annie and Emma shared. Nick thought about how comfortable and easy it had been to spend such a simple evening with Annie and Emma. Of course, he'd felt Annie's initial uneasiness when he accepted Emma's impulsive invitation to join them for Pizza Night, but once the three of them were seated at the table and laughing each time someone had finally been stuck with the Old Maid, Annie had become animated and genuine. Her smile and natural beauty were intoxicating to Nick, and just thinking about her brought a smile.

Nick had always quietly scoffed at anyone's declaration of *love at first sight*, but when he had met Annie and Emma the first time they came into the clinic and he'd seen Annie's blatant disdain for the clinic's dreary reception room, he had felt something inside that he had never felt before. Annie had blushed with embarrassment over letting her obvious disapproval of the tatty old reception area show on her face, and, well, that was when his skepticism vanished, and he had thought to himself, *So, this is what love at first sight feels like.*

Nonetheless, Dr. Chris understood the circumstances that had led Annie and Emma to his clinic. Annie's husband had died less than a year ago—Annie's sister, Jenny, had informed him of the accident the day she had made the appointment for Emma—so he knew there would have been no way Annie could have felt the same way upon first meeting him. It would take a long time for Annie Morgan to ever be able to feel *that* kind of connection with anyone, especially with him, Emma's therapist. But above and beyond his initial feelings about Annie, Dr. Chris could not shake away the feeling that his sister Lizzie was sitting beside him, whispering to him that his singular focus must be centered on Emma, just as it had been centered on Lizzie so long ago.

While Emma had been Dr. Chris's client for only a short amount of time, she had become his favorite appointment of each day. Undeniably, so many things about Emma reminded him of Lizzie: her smile, her determination, her childlike humor. One day, not long after Lizzie's accident, while Nick stretched and gently pulled Lizzie's arms and legs for what she had said was the hundredth time that day, she told him, "You are such a bossy doctor! I promise that I'm not going to call you Nick anymore. From now on I'm going to call you Dr. Chris!" And Lizzie had kept her promise, never again calling him Nick. But every one of Lizzie's 'Dr. Chris' references would be followed by a wink at her brother, a wink that expressed the deep love and gratitude she felt for him, a wink Nick would forever hold dear in memory of the sister he loved.

Over time, without being aware of it, Nick had developed a habit of winking. It was not really habitual or anything like a tick; in fact, his winks generally only occurred when he felt a strong connection with someone, and he definitely felt a strong connection with Emma. The first time she had attempted to return a little girl wink, his heart had melted, and he knew he would do everything he could to make her desire to once again walk become a reality.

The snowfall had stopped by the time Nick had driven his car into the clinic's parking lot after Pizza Night. After parking his car, he stood for a long moment looking at the three-story building he and his partners were restoring. He was temporarily living in one of the third-floor guest apartments that originally had been built for out-of-town guests of members of the athletic club, males only, of course. Now, even during the renovation, a guest apartment was the perfect set-up for Nick, not to mention its convenience and low cost. He didn't have to buy furniture, not even a bed. At a later date, all of the rooms would be renovated and turned into guest rooms for out-of-town patients and their family members. On the second floor, there was a full-service kitchen that the partners planned to turn into a café for their clients, offering smoothies made with fresh fruits and vegetables and other healthy options that would be organic, vegan and gluten-free. It all seemed pretty amazing to Nick.

The warm memory of being with Emma and Annie was still with him as he walked through the back entrance to the gym. He paused for a few moments in the dim light to admire the massive therapy space with the state-of-the-art equipment, and he felt a peacefulness in knowing that so many people, like Emma, would be helped here.

Earlier that week, Nick had spoken with Dr. Leonard twice to discuss the therapy Emma had previously received and to get his mentor's opinion about using the controversial Functional Electrical Stimulation, or FES. Dr. Leonard said he had not yet used it with Emma because her injury affected the nerves located between the first and second lumbar region of her spine. It was his considered opinion that because Emma had lost all sensation in her legs, any electrical stimulation would not be successful. He had also felt she was too young to receive the clinically unproven treatment.

During the conversation, Dr. Chris had disagreed with his former professor on one particular point, arguing that because Emma's injury had caused what was called "an incomplete spinal cord injury," there was a chance that with the use of FES, her damaged nerves might be able to re-generate, and some muscle function could be restored.

Moonlight Falls PT Clinic had all the financial backing they needed, thanks to their partner, Dr. Arnold, so they had been able to purchase the newest and best therapy equipment, including FES devices and a robotic "gaiter trainer" device. Dr. Chris was trained in how to use the FES devises in therapy and had wanted to prescribe the use of these for Emma's rehabilitation. He had briefly mentioned this new form of rehabilitation to Annie and Emma during their first tour of the clinic, explaining how Emma would have to be one hundred percent committed to a rigorous and demanding schedule five days a week, two hours each day, with extensive work at home every day. He had been careful to warn them that there was no guarantee regarding the outcome, but he had worked with some people with injuries like Emma's who had demonstrated measurable success in restoring some sensation and movement in their legs. He was inspired by the hopefulness he saw in Emma's eyes but worried about the concern he saw in Annie's.

Nick paused for a moment longer before turning off the lights to the gym and pressing the elevator button to the third floor. It had been a good day.

# CHAPTER 13

THE DELTA AIRLINES flight carrying Will Taylor touched down on a runway at the Minneapolis-St. Paul International Airport a few days before Christmas. As the plane taxied toward Lindberg Terminal, Will was pleased to see the familiar sight of snow-covered fields and pine trees, and he realized right then how grateful he was just to be alive. It was still highly improbable, he often thought, that when the undetected bomb exploded on that dusty road in Kandahar Province just three months ago, it had not killed him; instead, it had just shattered his left hip and femur.

The surgeries to replace his hip and insert a titanium rod inside his thigh bone had been successful, but his recovery was not over, not by a long shot. There would be many more months of therapy before undergoing another surgery to remove the titanium rod and then additional therapy would be needed before he would be able to put his full weight on his leg. Will was determined that when all was said and done, he would be able to walk without assistance and with a natural gait. That same resolve had caused him many moments of guilt, because he was already able to move his leg muscles and could put weight on his leg with the help of a walker, crutches or sometimes a cane, while at the same time, his niece, Emma, remained in a wheelchair with little hope of ever being able to walk again.

This was what Will was thinking about as an airport attendant wheeled him along the Gold Concourse leading to an elevator that would take him down to the baggage claim area, where he knew his parents would be waiting for him. He did not want them to see him in a wheelchair, but the airport personnel had insisted on it, ostensibly for insurance purposes, until he had reached the baggage carousel and could be released into the safekeeping of his family.

The closer Will got to the main terminal, the more anxious he became. If it hadn't been for the injuries, he would not have been able to come home for Christmas, so he was grateful to be spending the holidays at home with his family. But he was also worried that the memory of last Christmas would be too difficult for everyone. Even though he had not even been present last year to help Annie and Emma, his parents and Jenny had called him several times, just reaching out, intuitively knowing that Will was the emotional rock of the whole family and, therefore, needing his strength if only by voice or Skype. Even so, the memory of receiving the devastating news last December while stationed in Afghanistan was now haunting him. Like the rest of his family, he still carried pain and sorrow for Annie and Emma and knew that this year's celebration would not, *could not*, be the same joyful, carefree Christmas the Taylor family had always celebrated in all the years before the accident.

As his plans to come home had become firm, Will determined to do everything possible to make this Christmas meaningful and filled with all the healing and love the family desperately needed. He only hoped his buddy, who would be joining them, would be a welcomed addition, not a poorly conceived idea. Under the circumstances, Will would not have invited any of his other Army friends to this particular Christmas. But Jake was so unusual, so warm and accepting with nothing pretentious or insincere about him. Besides, Jake had no family to go home to for Christmas, and if any family would be able to embrace Jake, it was his own, despite the emotional pain his sister Annie would no doubt be feeling and the ongoing physical and emotional struggles of his niece, Emma.

An elevator door next to the baggage claim area opened, and an attendant pushed Will's wheelchair out the door and into the corridor leading to the baggage carousels. Almost immediately, Will saw his parents standing there, waiting for him, concerned looks on both of their faces.

Molly and Bill thought they had braced themselves for Will's arrival, but the shock of seeing their once strong and sturdy son now being wheeled toward where they were standing was overwhelming. As the wheelchair rolled to a stop, Will looked so gaunt and thin in his military uniform that Molly was unable to hide her emotions. She bit down on her lower lip as tears formed in her eyes.

"Hey, mom! None of that," said Will, fighting back his own emotions.

"Good to see you, son," said Bill Taylor as he leaned down and put his arms around Will, giving him a hug. Molly leaned in and became part of an impromptu, three-person hug.

"Mom, Dad!" Will wrapped his arms around both of them and broke into a broad, warm smile filled with love, happiness and relief at being home.

Molly began kissing his cheeks until Will laughed and said, "Mom, I can't breathe."

The attendant stepped forward. "Sir, it's been a pleasure assisting you. Would you like these now?" He held a pair of crutches in his hands.

"Definitely." With the help of the attendant Will lifted himself out of the chair and carefully stood on his right foot while settling the crutches under each arm. "Thank you!"

"No, I thank you, sir. Thank you for serving our country," said the attendant as he handed Bill a duffle bag filled with Will's belongings. "Merry Christmas, to all of you."

Molly and Bill both saw that the attendant wiped away tears from his eyes.

"Thanks again," said Will as the attendant turned and pushed the empty wheelchair back toward the elevator.

Bill looked extremely proud as he stood next to his son. After a moment, he looked around the baggage claim area, puzzled. "So, ah, where's your buddy?"

"He's been detained, but he'll be here in a few days," Will said.

"Great," said Bill. "Can't wait to meet him." He looked at the luggage carousel. "Any more bags?"

"Nope, that's it," said Will, pointing to the duffle bag.

"Well, okay then. We'd better get going. It's been snowing hard, so traffic will be extra slow."

"And Will, Jen and Sam and Annie and Emma are all coming over for dinner tonight," said Molly as she led the way to the exit, her son hobbling on crutches behind her. "They can't wait to see you!"

# CHAPTER 14

HOME HAD NEVER felt so good to Will. The house looked like Christmas itself, lighted on the outside, with the mini-herd of wire-reindeer having once again claimed their spot by the birch trees and the Steadfast Christmas Soldiers standing sentry on the front steps. Inside, Will was taken with all the garland and lights and the good smell of Christmas cookies and hot cider wafting from the kitchen and the scent of birchwood burning in the stone fireplace. He stood in the archway to the living room, leaning on his crutches. "Hey, Mom, what's with the Christmas tree? No lights?"

"We're all going to decorate it tonight. Just like old times."

"That's great."

Bill carried the duffle bag up to Will's bedroom, then came down the stairs to the living room. "I have to leave in a few minutes to pick up Emma and Annie," said Bill. "Annie's car's been in the repair shop for who-knows-how-long, so I'm taking them to Emma's physical therapy and then bringing them back here for dinner."

Molly looked at her son and put her hand on his cheek. "Why don't you go up to your room and take a rest. You've had a long day already."

Will kissed his mom's cheek, then turned to his dad. "How about if I pick up Annie and Emma? I'd like to surprise them."

"Sure you can drive?" Bill looked at Will's crutches that were supporting his weight on his left side.

Will smiled. "I don't drive with my left foot, so I'm good."

"Okay, here you go." Bill tossed the car keys to Will.

Annie opened her front door expecting to see her father. Instead, Will was standing there right before her eyes, smiling ear to ear, leaning on his crutches. "Is Emma home?" he asked with a tilt of his head.

Annie screamed and then began to cry. "Oh, Will!" She carefully smothered him with hugs and kisses before calling out, "Emma, come see who's here!"

The day Emma was born was the day Will's heart burst with a love he'd never felt before, and he instantly became the uncle every child deserves, doting on her endlessly and celebrating, along with Ron and Annie, every milestone Emma accomplished. This was his precious niece, his godchild, and there was nothing he wouldn't do for her.

"Uncle Willy!" Emma cried out in joy.

Will was alarmed as he watched Emma wheel herself toward him and Annie. Emma had still been in the hospital when Will made his brief visit last January, and while he had visited her, she had been heavily sedated and was unaware of his presence. Prior to that it had been almost eighteen months since he had been home visiting and had chased Emma around Annie and Ron's spacious backyard. How did it happen that six-year-old Emma looked more grown up, less childlike? Had the events of the past year stolen her youthfulness?

Will handed his crutches to Annie, leaned down to hug Emma

and then gently took her face into his hands. "This can't be my Emma Bannemma."

Emma giggled. She loved Will's nickname for her. "Yes, it is!" Emma giggled again and then took Will's face into her own hands and kissed his nose.

"Oh my, you look so beautiful and so grown up! What have you been doing while I was away?"

"I've been doing a lot of physical therapy." She looked down at her legs. "I think my legs are getting stronger."

"Good girl!" Will gave Emma another kiss on the cheek and then straightened up using only his right leg. He held up the car keys. "Hey, guess who's taking you and your mom to therapy today."

"You?" Emma said hopefully.

"Yep. Me. I begged Grandpa to let me be a pinch-driver for him. So, let's get this show on the road."

As they rode to therapy, Will teased Annie for letting the maintenance go on her van to the point that it needed to be towed and was now quarantined in the repair shop, waiting for replacement parts to arrive. As hard as Annie tried to redeem herself, Will kept teasing her and making Emma laugh. Annie loved how Will always had a way of finding the humor in most of life's obstacles and hindrances.

"Wow, looks like they really did a number on the old club," said Will as he wheeled Emma from the parking lot toward the clinic's entrance.

"Wait 'til you see the inside," said Annie as they entered the reception area.

Dr. Chris was waiting for them and immediately perceived their cheerful state of mind.

"Dr. Chris, this is my brother, Will," Annie said.

"Uncle Willy," Emma corrected.

Will reached out to shake hands with the doctor. "Uncle Willy only to my favorite niece."

"It's a pleasure to meet you, Will," said Dr. Chris. "Welcome home."

"Thanks. Great to be here."

Annie had noticed how Dr. Chris glanced at Emma with one of his signature winks. Emma had quickly smiled back with a more practiced wink of her own, which warmed Annie's heart.

"Let's get started; what do you say, Emma?" asked Dr. Chris.

"I say let's roll," said Emma, grabbing the wheels of her wheelchair and rolling herself toward the gym.

Annie was grateful to have had Will present during Emma's entire therapy session, since he had been through extensive therapy himself. During each exercise, Will asked Dr. Chris questions regarding its purpose and intended result, even as Emma had strained with super-human effort on each one. For Annie, it had always been so hard to watch Emma struggle with all her might, never whimpering or crying out in pain. But she was glad to have Will there, asking questions and forming a natural bond with Emma's therapist.

By the time the therapy lesson was over, Emma was in the happiest of spirits and out of nowhere, she blurted out, "Dr. Chris, we're going to my grandma and grandpa's house for dinner because Uncle Willy is home. Can you come too?"

"Oh, my goodness, Emma, sweetie, Dr. Chris has other—"

"Yes. Why don't you join us," said Will, interrupting Annie. "My parents always have way too much food, and I'd actually like to talk to you about something and get your opinion."

"Well, it sounds like an offer I shouldn't refuse," said Dr. Chris. "But I do have another therapy session." He noticed instant disappointment on Emma's face, so with a wink in her direction he continued. "But if it's all right, I could come after that. Would that be okay?"

"Yes!" shouted Emma so loud that other patients in the gym looked at them.

# CHAPTER 15

THE QUIET SOUND of holiday music and a glow from the fireplace filled Bill and Molly Taylor's living room with warmth and tranquility. Annie was seated on the hardwood floor beside Emma's wheelchair, next to the Christmas tree. From the boxes her father and Sam had hauled in from the garage, Annie carefully unwrapped ornaments and handed them to Emma for her to place on the lower boughs of the Christmas tree. Standing on a stepladder, unplugged strands of lights dangling around his neck, Bill waited for Molly to hand him the star that had topped their Christmas trees for more than forty years. Perched on the sofa, his injured leg resting on an ottoman, Will watched the happy, bumbling tree-trimming activities as he attempted to untangle yet another snarled string of tree lights.

From the kitchen, Jenny called out, "I think the roast needs another fifteen minutes, Mom."

"Oh, goodness," said Molly as she handed the star to her husband. "I'd better finish up the vegetables. Emmy, would you like to help me with the mashed potatoes?"

"Yes!" Emma loved helping her grandmother cook, especially because Annie rarely cooked anymore. They mainly ate frozen casseroles and take-out food and lots of raw vegetables dipped in ranch dressing, because Annie didn't like to take the time to steam or boil them.

Emma coaxed her wheelchair in the direction of the kitchen and disappeared with her grandmother.

Annie looked at the grandfather clock standing sentry in a prominent location across the room. It was after seven, and she was wondering if Dr. Chris had decided not to come. At this moment, she was actually hoping he would not arrive. After all, Emma had put him in an awkward position by extending another invitation to him without first asking Annie if it was okay. Just as Annie had convinced herself that the good doctor would not be joining them this evening, the doorbell rang. Annie quietly moaned.

Bill hurried down the step ladder and walked over to the front door. "Dr. Chris! Great to meet you. Emma talks about you nonstop! I feel like we've already met—I'm Bill Taylor, Emma's grandpa."

"Nice to meet you," said Dr. Chris as the two men shook hands. "Nick Christopher."

"We've been hearing 'Doctor Chris' so often that I'm not sure I can revert to just Nick, but either way, I'm glad you could join us." Bill gestured for Dr. Chris to hang his jacket on an old-fashioned hat rack strategically placed in the foyer. "Come on in and meet the rest of the family," added Bill, escorting Dr. Chris toward the living room. With his warm and comfortable way with people, it was easy to see why Bill had enjoyed a successful career in public relations.

Emma rolled her wheelchair out of the kitchen in a hurry to greet *her* guest. "Hi, Doctor Chris," said Emma as she rolled toward him.

"Hi there, Emma!" he said in response.

Jenny and Molly had followed behind Emma, wiping their

hands on their aprons, while Annie lingered by the Christmas tree, watching as Dr. Chris received the customary Taylor family reception—always warm and welcoming.

"These are for you." Dr. Chris offered a potted, red poinsettia to Molly.

"Thank you so much," said Molly, graciously accepting the gift. "Very nice to meet you."

"And you," said Dr. Chris. "What a beautiful home."

"Thank you," said Molly. "We love it."

"Dr. Chris, come see the Christmas tree!" Emma took Dr. Chris' hand while allowing her grandfather to push her wheelchair into the living room. "We're not done decorating it, so you can help us." Emma looked happy and proud to have *her* Dr. Chris meet her family.

Throughout the rest of the evening Annie calmly observed the ease with which her family included Dr. Chris in every conversation and activity. It was enjoyable, and she was happy for everyone. But for Annie, there was a deep and unyielding sadness that reminded her that this night should have been different. Ron should have been at their table laughing and telling stories, and Emma should be dancing around the room, not confined to a wheelchair.

"Uncle Willy," Emma said just as Will took a bite of the chocolate cake Molly had made for dessert to celebrate his homecoming. "There's someone missing tonight."

Annie froze, worried that Emma had read her mind, that she would say that her daddy was the someone who was missing. The entire family must have thought the same thing, since the room suddenly fell silent.

"Isn't your Army buddy supposed to be here?" asked Emma, looking at Will.

Annie felt the tension in the room disappear.

"Not yet, kiddo." Will finished chewing a mouthful of cake. "He won't be here until Christmas Eve Day. His doctors wouldn't release him from the hospital until then."

"Did he get hurt as bad as you?" Emma asked.

"Actually, he got the worst of it, Emmy. He lost his left leg, but he's going to be fine with some more therapy."

"Just like you and me," Emma said cheerfully. "Dr. Chris and I can help your buddy with his exercises!" said Emma, smiling at the doctor.

"Emma, you will be the best medicine my buddy Jake could ever ask for," said Will, proudly smiling at his beloved niece. Then he turned to look at everyone seated at the table. "He's gonna love being here for Christmas."

Emma suddenly became visibly upset. She put her hands in her lap and stared at her dinner plate. "But Mommy and I aren't going to be here. We're going to Orlando for Christmas." A lone tear rolled down her cheek.

Will looked at Annie for confirmation. Annie nodded, feeling the blood drain from her face. *Great, another reason to feel guilty... for what? For not wanting to relive last Christmas. For wanting to ease her daughter's pain... and her own?*

"Don't worry, Emmy," Will leaned over, took his niece's hand into his own and kissed it. "Jake will be here when you get back from your vacation."

"Promise?"

"I promise."

Annie quietly wiped her mouth with her napkin, placed it on the table and slowly stood up. "It's been a wonderful dinner, Mom and Dad, but it's getting late, and Emma and I should be getting home." The moment Annie had said those words, she remembered she didn't have a car. She first looked at her father, then at Will, hoping one of them would jump to the occasion.

"It's getting late for me, too," Dr. Chris said before Will or Bill could respond. He looked at Annie. "I'd be happy give you and Emma a ride home."

"Oh, umm," Annie stammered, having been caught off guard.

"It's no problem. Really. I'm heading that direction," said Dr. Chris as he stood up from his chair.

"That's perfect!" Emma blurted out and rolled herself away from the table as if the matter had been settled once and for all.

"Well—" Annie was uncomfortable about accepting the offer from Dr. Chris, but her father looked tired, as did Will. "Okay. Thank you, that would be nice."

It was a good thing she had accepted his offer, thought Annie as she and Emma were once again being driven home by Dr. Chris. The snow had not stopped falling since early afternoon, and the streets had not yet been plowed, so the drive home was slow and challenging. Emma, not at all concerned about the precarious drive, chatted endlessly from the backseat of the car, recounting everything about therapy earlier in the day and their wonderful dinner together at her grandparents' house and how great it was that Dr. Chris could come and help decorate the tree, until finally Dr. Chris pulled up in front of their house. For a moment, both Emma and Annie thought he had driven into the wrong driveway.

"Mommy! Look!" Emma squealed with amazement. "There are Christmas lights all along our front porch and around our front door!" Emma exhaled with ecstasy. "And there are Christmas lights all around my tree, the one Daddy and I always decorated together!"

"Oh my," was all Annie could muster as she gazed at her

front yard and quietly took in the splendor of the colorful Christmas lights.

"Who do you think did this, Mommy?" Emma's face showed such joy and wonder.

Annie questioningly tilted her head at Dr. Chris who offered a slight smile as he shrugged his shoulders with feigned innocence.

"I don't know, sweetie."

Emma looked toward the sky, "I know who it was." Her voice sounded angelic. "It was Daddy. Daddy did this because he didn't want us to have Christmas without him."

Annie's heart broke in half. "Yes, Emmy," said Annie as she looked at Dr. Chris and smiled. "I think you're right."

Dr. Chris gave her a quick half-wink and a warm smile.

Annie stepped out of the front seat, opened the back door and lifted Emma into her arms. The two hugged each other, and Emma's head nestled into Annie's neck as Annie carried her daughter up the snowy sidewalk to their house.

Dr. Chris followed behind, pushing Emma's wheelchair. At the front door, he gently placed Emma into the chair, then turned to Annie. She looked at him, almost as if looking into his eyes for the first time. She placed her hand on Nick's arm. "Thank you," she said, then turned and wheeled Emma into the house.

"Goodnight," said Dr. Chris to both Annie and Emma. He hesitated just for a moment, looked at the beautiful Christmas lights framing the house, then walked down the snowy path toward his car, feeling a lightness in his step.

# CHAPTER 16

THE MORNING AFTER the Taylors' tree decorating party, the reception room of the Moonlight Falls PT Clinic was in a minor state of chaos. White tarps covered the newly laid flooring as two men on ladders painted the crown molding and two others, on their knees, painted the floorboards. Jenny was standing in the middle of the room, inspecting the work and reviewing with Dr. Chris the timetable for the arrival of the new furniture, when Annie and Emma arrived for Emma's therapy session.

"Oooo, Aunt Jenny the room looks so happy," Emma said while taking in the almost-completed remodeling and decorating.

"I'm so glad you like it, Emm," said Jenny. "Just wait until we're done!" Jenny had picked out a soft garden-green color for the walls in the waiting area and a soft blue-green hue for the area surrounding the receptionist's desk. Jenny had told Dr. Chris that green was considered the color of harmony and renewal, echoing the hues of the natural world.

"I could stay here forever," said Emma as she inhaled a deep breath of air filled with the scent of fresh paint.

"Well, I like hearing that, but you and I have some work to do in the gym," Dr. Chris said as he and reached for her wheelchair handles. "So, away we go."

Annie turned to follow them into the gym.

"Annie, can you stay here for a minute?" asked Jenny. "I want to talk to you about tonight."

"Sure." Annie smiled at her daughter. "I'll be with you in a minute, Emm."

Emma looked over her shoulder. "Aunt Jenny, I'm bringing a new toy for Tom," she said while being wheeled out of the reception room.

"Tom will be so happy. See you later!" Jenny called out just as the gym door closed.

Inside the gym, Dr. Chris carefully pushed Emma's wheelchair over to one of the therapy tables. "So, who is this Tom?" Dr. Chris asked.

"Tom is Aunt Jenny's cat, and he loves any fuzzy mouse toy! Mommy and I got him a new one."

"Lucky Tom," said Dr. Chris as one of his assistants helped him lift Emma onto a platform table. They positioned her so that she was seated with her back straight, leaning against a support apparatus.

"I'm going to have a sleepover tonight with Aunt Jenny, and we're going to make Christmas cookies," said Emma.

"Sounds fun and delicious."

"What are *you* doing tonight?" asked Emma as Dr. Chris stretched out her legs.

"Oh, I have to tell you, my evening is not nearly as exciting as yours and your mommy's. I'm going to do a little paperwork, and then I'll probably walk over to the Old Town Café across the street. They have pretty good hamburgers and really good milkshakes."

Emma was positioned with her back securely harnessed to the

table and her legs straightened flat on the table's surface. She had a very solemn look on her face.

"My mommy's not coming to the sleepover. It's just me and Aunt Jenny."

"What about your Uncle?"

"No, silly. It's a *girls' only* sleepover. Besides, Uncle Sam had to fly to Chicago this morning for a meeting."

"Ohhhh, I see," Dr. Chris said as he began attaching round patches to Emma's left thigh.

"I'm worried that Mommy will be sad being alone tonight." Emma furrowed her brow and frowned.

Dr. Chris connected the patches to cables that would carry electric pulses to Emma's spinal nerves and her leg muscles.

"Well, I'm sure your mom has all sorts of plans and will be happy knowing you're having fun with your aunt." As he spoke, he rolled a square control box closer to the therapy table and began to enter some numbers using its keypad.

"Nooo," Emma said, slowly shaking her head. "She doesn't have any plans."

Dr. Chris continued to type on the keypad.

Emma suddenly shouted out. "Dr. Chris!"

He looked up at her, startled, afraid she was experiencing some pain.

Emma's eyes widened, as if being hit with a sudden brainstorm. "Mommy loves hamburgers and milkshakes! You could take Mommy out for dinner tonight... and then she won't feel so alone... and I won't feel so sad for her... and then I can have a happy time with Aunt Jenny!" Emma sounded excited and hopeful.

"Ah, well, hmm," he stammered, then broke into a nervous smile as he saw Annie enter the gym.

"Hi, guys," Annie said cheerfully as she approached them. "How's everything going?"

"Great!" Emma had a very big smile on her face. "Guess what!"

Dr. Chris turned his attention to the keypad.

Annie laughed at how excited her daughter seemed. "What, you silly girl?"

"You aren't busy tonight and Dr. Chris isn't busy either, so he's going to take you out for dinner at the Old Town Café, so you won't be alone while I'm with Aunt Jenny."

Both Annie and Dr. Chris looked at Emma, their mouth's gaping. In unison, they turned to look at each other, then quickly looked back at Emma who was smiling with the forced innocence of a skillful conniver.

"Emma?" Annie said with a firm parental tone.

Emma's smile withered when she saw the look on her mother's face, a clear sign that she had crossed the line this time. Emma looked down at her lap to avoid eye contact with her mother. "I told Dr. Chris that you like milkshakes, too," she said quietly.

"Oh, my goodness," Annie looked mortified as she turned again to face Dr. Chris. "I am so sorry."

"You know, I'm actually a little tired of eating hamburgers and milkshakes all alone." Dr. Chris scratched the back of his neck and sheepishly smiled at Annie. "The truth is, I've been holding off eating at that new restaurant on Town Square, because it seems too nice to dine there all alone." He opened the palms of his hands and hunched his shoulders, waiting for Annie to respond. Instead, she kept him dangling, so he changed his tone and addressed her directly. "Annie, would you join me for dinner tonight at Francesca's?" He smiled at Annie, then continued. "That is, if—"

"Hmm," Annie said with a smile, knowing all along that she would accept his offer. "Thank you. That would be very nice."

"Yay! It's a date!" Emma shouted and raised her arms in victory.

# CHAPTER 17

FROM THE MOMENT Annie opened her front door to greet Dr. Chris, she felt ill at ease and awkward like a teenager on her first date. "Hi," she said, knowing she sounded stiff and nervous.

"Hi," Dr. Chris said with a warm smile. Annie looked striking in a black dress and high-heeled shoes. She looked so beautiful that Dr. Chris had trouble finding any more words.

"So..." Annie remained standing in the doorway with her wool coat draped over her arm.

"So..." Dr. Chris echoed, showing a little nervousness himself. He stepped forward to help Annie put on her wool coat.

"Oh, thank you." The manner in which Dr. Chris pulled her coat over her shoulders, the way he let his hands rest there for a brief second felt, well... so very... *so very pleasurable.*

"Ready?" Dr. Chris asked.

"Yes." Annie fumbled with her purse and then fumbled with an apology. "I'm sorry you had to pick me up. I would have met you at the restaurant if my car wasn't still in the garage... that darn thingamajig that I managed to destroy is taking forever to arrive."

Dr. Chris laughed. "Thingamajigs always take a long time to arrive. You know why that is, don't you?"

Annie looked at the tall and handsome Dr. Chris. "No, I have no idea. Why is that?"

"Well, everyone knows thingamajigs are made in the deepest part of outer Mongolia."

Momentarily surprised by Dr. Chris's wit, Annie laughed heartily but was not about to be outdone. She looked him in the eye and said, "And thingamajigs can only be flown here by the great Mongolian Swan Goose."

"Who happens to be vacationing in Siberia until the new year," Dr. Chris retorted. They both laughed at their unplanned repartee as he gently placed his hand on Annie's back and led her to his car.

Francesca's Ristorante, located just across from Town Square in a building that once was a large real estate office, had opened earlier in the fall and had quickly become the most popular restaurant in town. It was owned by Francesca Vitalli-Pickney, a beautiful Italian woman in her mid-forties, and her husband, Robert Pickney, a blue-blooded stockbroker from Lake Minnetonka, an exclusive suburb west of Minneapolis. Last May, Francesca and Robert had driven through Moonlight Falls on a Sunday afternoon drive, and after doing some research they realized there were a few good cafés and diners in the area but not one world-class restaurant within miles. As if having an epiphany, Francesca envisioned an opportunity to create something different, a place with the ambience of a Tuscany Ristorante and the authentic Italian cuisine of her homeland. Francesca's Ristorante had opened in early October and very quickly had become a favorite of locals and visitors alike.

Annie and Dr. Chris were led by a young, dark-haired maitre d' to a cozy, candlelit table next to a window that looked out on Town Square. With *old-world* manners, the young man pulled out Annie's chair and waited for her to take a seat, then nodded for

Dr. Chris to settle into his. He then handed each of them a large, leather-bound menu. "Carlo will be your waiter this evening. *Buon Appetito!*" he said before turning to leave.

"*Buon Appetito,*" Dr. Chris said to Annie with a nervous smile.

"Yes, well, same to you." Annie knew her comment probably sounded a little rude, so she picked up the leather-bound menu and raised it high enough to cover her face.

"Thank you, I think," said Dr. Chris.

An awkward moment of silence filled the air as both Annie and Dr. Chris pretended to be surveying the menu items.

"So, who is this Alfredo of Alfredo pasta, Alfredo chicken, Alfredo shrimp?" asked Dr. Chris.

Annie peered over the top of her menu to see Dr. Chris grinning at her. "I was just wondering the same thing, and you know what?"

"What?"

"I'd like to know just why Mr. Alfredo's fettuccini is listed *Especial* when the other Alfredos aren't."

And it went from there, as Annie and Dr. Chris each rifted off the other's comments until other patrons started looking their way, wondering what was so amusing about the menu the couple near the window was reading.

"Stop! My checks hurt," said Annie still laughing as she put her napkin to her lips.

By the time Francesca herself came to their table with their Panzanella Salads, Annie and Nick had covered all of the obvious subjects—Emma's progress, their pasts, Annie's college life and her career in marketing; and Nick's childhood in suburban New York, his college life and medical school, and how much they both loved Moonlight Falls.

"So, you and Emma are spending Christmas in Orlando," said Dr. Chris.

"We are. I'm looking forward to it, and so is Emma—at least I thought she was," said Annie. She looked out the window, gazing at the Christmas lights twinkling from the pine trees on Town Square. "But now, I'm not so sure. She's become a little more aloof about the whole get-away-to-Florida plan." Annie tilted her head slightly and looked at Dr. Chris, as if hoping for some words of wisdom. "I know it's odd when everyone else in the world wants to be with family at this time of year, and here I am wanting to be as far away from family as I... as Emmy and I can get. It must seem crazy."

"Not at all."

Annie held onto her glass of red wine and looked at it as if it were a psychic's crystal ball. "It just seems like the right thing to do... after what happened last Christmas." Her voice trailed off, and she looked up at Dr. Chris.

To her surprise, he gently put his hand on hers. "Annie don't be so hard on yourself. It is the right thing to do. You're a wise woman and a very good mother. I think you and Emma will have a happy and healing time together."

Annie looked down at the hand that covered hers and gratefully accepted the intended kindness.

A waiter approached their table and quietly whisked away their salad plates while Annie and Dr. Chris each reached for their glasses of wine. Within moments, a second waiter appeared with dishes of Pasta al'Amatriciana.

"These plates are very hot," warned the waiter in a slight Italian accent as he set the first plate in front of Annie and the second in front of Dr. Chris. *"Buon appetito."*

"Thank you," said Annie to the waiter. Then she looked at Dr. Chris with a warm smile. "This looks delicious. *Buon Appetito!*"

Throughout their meal together, Annie and Dr. Chris commented on the extraordinary taste of the pasta and the wonderful aromas that filled the room. Maybe it was the ambiance of Francesca's and the intimacy of a quiet table nestled by the window overlooking Town Square, or maybe it was their frequent laughs or the occasional locking onto each other's eyes that allowed the two of them to feel safe enough to slowly share with each other the intimate details of their separate tragedies and the pain and heartbreak that follows such things.

But there was something else, something barely discernible but clearly magical that made the evening at Francesca's go by too quickly for both Annie and Dr. Chris. Without even knowing it, over an exquisite dinner at a romantic Italian restaurant, their doctor-client relationship transformed into something quite different.

# CHAPTER 18

A FEW DAYS before Christmas, Molly was sitting at the kitchen table with two empty packing boxes placed at her feet. The word **DONATION** had been written in black marker on one of the boxes and the word **KEEP/KITCHEN** had been written on the other. Various pots and pans were piled high on the kitchen counter along with assorted cooking utensils. Bill walked into the room, then slowly came to a stop as he saw his wife staring with blank eyes at the disarray.

Molly turned and looked at Bill, holding her right index finger to her lips, quietly shushing him, then pointed toward the family room. Bill tiptoed to the doorway to take a closer look and saw Will sound asleep on the sofa, his injured leg resting on the ottoman, his crutches propped against the adjacent rocking chair. To Bill, his son looked like a boy of about fourteen or fifteen, just coming into manhood, not yet ready to face the world. He looked angelic, too, not at all like a seasoned combat veteran.

Returning to the kitchen, Bill sat down at the table and looked at Molly, still wondering to himself how a boy so young could have already been injured in combat. "Hey," he whispered to his wife, glancing at the boxes in front of her. "I thought we weren't going to start packing until after Christmas." He looked sternly at Molly, concerned about her doing anything physical, especially since she had just completed her final chemotherapy treatment and her last CT scan. They both knew she should be taking it easy. Christmas was stressful enough.

"I know. I just feel restless and thought I'd get a little bit of a head start. Trouble is, I can't decide what to pack up and what to give away." Molly looked overwhelmed and weary, as if she had just been put in checkmate, having run out of options, unable to make a move.

Bill pulled his chair a little closer to Molly and put his arm around her shoulders, inhaling the scent of the apple cider simmering on the stove. "Well babe, I can tell you that we definitely don't need to keep that!" Bill said in a loud whisper as he pointed toward a gaudy, bright yellow and black sunflower tea kettle that had always been hidden at the bottom of a seldom-opened kitchen drawer.

Molly giggled. "I would love to give it away, but it was a gift from your cousin Jane, and you know she always asks for a cup of tea when she's visiting… just to be sure I still have it."

"Well, we're going to move to a smaller place with far less storage space," Bill kept his voice as low as he could. "So, as much as I will miss the old teapot, I vote to throw it into the giveaway box."

Molly giggled again and burrowed her head into Bill's neck. From the family room, they heard Will stirring in his sleep, trying to adjust his leg.

Bill waited a moment to be certain Will was still sleeping. "Molly Dolly," he said softly into her ear. "We can hire people to help us pack."

"But they won't know what to keep and what to give away. They won't know what has meaning and what doesn't. We've lived here almost all of our married life and—"

"One step at a time, Mol," interrupted Bill. "We always knew the day would come when we'd have to downsize."

In truth, Bill had never really believed a day would come when they would need to give up their house. He'd always imagined them living in their dream home until the day they died. But when Molly was diagnosed with stage four cancer, with the odds stacked against her surviving another two to five years, he had begun to think that a change might be necessary. And then, when the opportunity came out of the blue to sell the drafty old house, Bill felt certain it was in Molly's best interest to move somewhere with fewer rooms to clean and fewer stairs to climb, a place with a smaller garden to tend and less of a yard for either of them to worry about. And if needed, somewhere closer to the medical center. Just in case.

Molly had let Bill's words settle for a moment, then she took a deep breath followed by an audible sigh. "I never really thought the day would come, but you're right, darling, it's probably time, and how wonderful it is to know that such a sweet, young couple wants to start their own family right here where we started ours."

"Still, I have moments when I wonder if we're doing the right thing," said Bill, his voice revealing more than a hint of seller's remorse.

"No, you're right," Molly said firmly. "We are doing the right thing." Molly felt tired and weak from the chemo, and if it weren't a few days before Christmas, she would have retreated to their bedroom for a nap. "You know, it will be easier for us to live in a one-story home, where you won't have so much upkeep with all the things that go wrong with a house this old." Molly knew Bill had always enjoyed tending to the issues that popped up. He relished figuring out how to replace the basement pipes, repair the roof and unclog the kitchen and bathroom drains. But she worried that, should she need further treatment for the cancer, or worse, the house would be too much for him to handle.

"You're right, as usual," said Bill, smiling lovingly at his wife. "We aren't getting any younger and neither is this house." Bill sounded like he was trying to convince himself that moving would be the best thing for both of them.

"I just wish we could have this one last Christmas here with Annie and Jenny and Sam and Will and especially Emma. Otherwise, our most lasting memories of Christmas in our home will be of last Christmas when—" Molly's voice trailed off, leaving the unmentionable unmentioned.

They both sat quietly for a moment until Molly broke the silence. "I understand why Annie needs to take Emma to Orlando, and I was all for it until we accepted the offer on our home. Now I think Annie and Emma need to be here for the very same reason Annie doesn't want to be here."

The sound of Bill's cell phone interrupted their discussion. He looked to see who it was, then said to Molly, "This might be important. Do you mind if I take this call?"

Molly nodded to Bill and watched him walk toward his office and close the door. Molly continued to worry about Annie and Emma until her own cell phone buzzed. She hesitated for a moment before answering. "Hello? Yes, of course I can wait." Molly slowly stood up while gripping tightly to the cell.

"Hello, Dr. Olsen," Molly said quietly into the phone, turning her back so no one could hear her. Molly fell silent as she listened to the caller.

"I see," Molly said as she covered her mouth with her hand and closed her eyes.

She listened for a moment more and then ended the call. "Yes, I'll make that appointment with your scheduler. Goodbye."

Molly looked at the mess of pots and pans, then picked up

the ugly sunflower tea pot and placed it in the moving box with the label **DONATION**. "Well, I guess that's that," Molly said and slowly walked to the back porch and disappeared.

Molly and Bill had been wrong in thinking that Will was asleep while they were whispering to each other in the adjoining kitchen. He'd only been dozing and had overheard most of what his parents had discussed. He also overheard his mother's call from her doctor and while he'd not seen the look on her face as she received the news, Will knew the meaning behind her whisper when he heard her say, "Well, I guess that's that." His heart sank. He lay quietly on the sofa deep in thought for what may have been a full minute. When he finally decided what needed to be done, he reached for his crutches, carefully hoisted himself up and off the couch, and hobbled into the kitchen.

He quickly scribbled a note on a yellow post-it: "I went to Annie's for a little while. See you for dinner. Will." He stuck the note on the refrigerator door, grabbed the car keys from the kitchen counter and made his way into the mudroom and out the back door.

PART FOUR

# CHRISTMAS HOPE

# CHAPTER 19

JENNY HAD AWAKENED early in the morning feeling nauseous and achy. At first, she wasn't worried, because she had read somewhere that nausea signaled a rise in hormone levels and a rise in hormones meant a lower risk of miscarriage. Jenny had experienced nausea in a previous pregnancy but had miscarried anyway, so she was cautious about feeling hopeful this time. But very quickly she began to feel back pain and then the familiar low-level contractions that had always occurred before her previous miscarriages.

Sam called her doctor and was told to take Jenny to the Valley Hospital emergency room. It was all too familiar, and they had learned bitter lessons in the past.

A few years ago, within hours of learning about her first pregnancy, Jenny and Sam had told family and friends and anyone who happened to be within shouting distance about their expected baby. Jenny had loved telling little Emma, who was a toddler at the time, that she was going to have a cousin, and Jenny, being Type-A *and* an interior decorator, had already begun to transform an upstairs bedroom into a nursery. But shortly after the walls had been painted a soft sea-foam green and an ivory colored crib with a matching changing table had been added to the nursery, Jenny had suffered a miscarriage. As devastating as that was, Jenny and Sam were hopeful when the doctor told them to try again, that the likelihood of another miscarriage was slim.

Six months later, Jenny had become pregnant again, and even though they felt some apprehension given the recent past, Jenny and Sam couldn't stop themselves from sharing their joy and excitement with family and friends. After all, hadn't the doctor said there was little risk of another miscarriage? Eleven weeks into that pregnancy, and one day after Jenny had purchased a glider chair and ottoman for the nursery, she miscarried again.

After that, Jenny and Sam had both begun to show signs of clinical depression. Neither of them had been able to get a full night of sleep. They began shying away from family and friends and even when they were with others, they seemed edgy and stressed. Together Jenny and Sam made several treks to a fertility clinic to be tested in search of any biological reason that might be causing the miscarriages, but nothing showed up on either side that would explain the "why" of their situation. So, they kept trying, and within the year Jenny was once again pregnant. This time around, Jenny and Sam told only their immediate family and did not share the news with any friends or colleagues. It was just as well, for Jenny once again miscarried before the tenth week of that pregnancy.

Discouraged by that last turn of events, and even more about the stress on their relationship, they decided to meet with a marriage counselor to help with their grief. The counseling sessions led Jenny and Sam to the decision to try one last time to have a child. Then came the Christmas Eve accident last year. They put their plans on hold, knowing Annie and Emma would both need Jenny's help in the aftermath of the accident.

Eight months had passed before Annie had been able to say she could now structure her life with Emma in such a way as to not need as much of Jenny's help day-to-day. So, when Jenny had once again become pregnant, she and Sam had kept the news to themselves. No need to worry anyone or get everyone's hopes up unless and until Jenny's pregnancy reached twenty weeks. That would not be until just before Christmas.

They had almost made it. Jenny had reached week nineteen with no signs of trouble. But on the day Will had overheard his mom's conversation with her doctor and had gone to Annie's house, Sam had once again rushed Jenny to the hospital.

Several hours later, Jenny and Sam sat in their car numb and silent while waiting for the traffic light to change. When the light turned green, Sam nudged the car forward in silence. They could find no words to describe how they were feeling.

Even after Sam had turned into their driveway and turned off the car motor, the two remained in the front seat, staring out the window. They didn't look at each other and they didn't say a word until Jenny broke the silence.

"Sam, tomorrow I'm going to change the nursery."

Sam nodded and said quietly, "I understand."

"And Sam, I don't want to tell anyone until after Christmas, not until Annie and Emma get back from Orlando."

Sam reached for Jenny's hand and held it tightly. "Okay," he said, barely holding his emotions in check.

# CHAPTER 20

THAT SAME MORNING, as Jenny and Sam were rushing to the hospital, Annie was kneeling next to the wheelchair to put on Emma's snow boots. They were about to head to the clinic for Emma's therapy.

"Mommy, do you know what Dr. Chris says?"

"No. What does Dr. Chris say?" Annie looked at her daughter.

"Dr. Chris says that my brain is sending messages to my leg muscles and my legs are trying to listen."

Annie said, "That's very interesting."

"Do you want to know what I told Dr. Chris?"

"What."

"I told Dr. Chris that he needs to get hearing aids for my legs."

Annie laughed so hard that tears welled up in her eyes, and when she reached out to hug Emma, she realized that it had been a very long time since she and Emma had shared a true, spontaneous and unforced kind of laughter.

Emma was scheduled to have an hour-long aqua therapy session before her session with Dr. Chris, so Annie decided to use the time to walk down Main Street, get some fresh air and maybe drop into one or two of the shops.

She had not felt an ounce of Christmas spirit this year, that is, not until Emma and she had discovered the Christmas lights in their front yard and Annie had seen the joy in Emma's face. At first, Annie had assumed Will had been the one to fill her front yard with twinkling lights, *but then, hadn't Dr. Chris winked at her when Emma asked who had done it?* Still, Annie preferred to believe, along with Emma, that Ron had somehow performed a minor Christmas miracle in their own front yard.

Annie strolled past several shops, each one with window displays shouting out Christmas cheer. No one in the family had expected Annie to buy Christmas gifts this year, and she truly had not even thought of buying gifts for anyone; she just didn't have it within her. The Orlando trip was designed to replace any Christmas presents for Emma and herself, and Emma seemed to understand the trade-off, since she had not once asked to see Santa, nor had she written him a letter with a list of things she wanted. Last year, she had wanted a new bicycle, but then…..

Annie stopped in front the gift shop where she used to find all sorts of unique gifts for just about anyone. She stared at the window for a few minutes and then decided to go inside just to get out of the cold and maybe find something for her parents—nothing extravagant, just something meaningful… and maybe she'd get something small for Will, even though he seemed pretty upset with her the other day when he came by hoping to convince her to stay in Moonlight Falls for Christmas—as he said, for their mother's sake. Browsing, she had also begun to think of buying something for Jenny and Sam, even though Annie felt that Jenny had been avoiding her calls, and then when Jenny did answer her cell phone, her responses were curt and brief. Annie assumed this was because Will had told Jenny that Annie had not canceled the trip to Orlando and, furthermore, would not be canceling it.

Emma had just completed a series of stretches with Dr. Chris and was feeling especially excited about what they had accomplished in the last few days.

"Dr. Chris, Christmas Eve is in two days," said Emma.

"You are right, Emma. And what a special Christmas Eve you and your mommy are going to have."

"Do you know what we usually do on Christmas Eve?"

"No," said Dr. Chris while he unfastened the electrical vest Emma wore around her waist.

"Well, that's when everyone goes to Grandma and Grandpa's house, and we sit around the Christmas tree, and we each get to open just one present.

"Just one?"

"Yep.

And then we go to church, which is really nice. Then on Christmas Day, we get to open all our other presents."

"I like that."

"Do you know what I would give Mommy on Christmas Eve if we were at Grandma and Grandpa's this year?"

"Tell me."

Emma cupped her hands over Dr. Chris' ear and whispered.

"Emma, I think that would be such a wonderful present," said Dr. Chris, clearly surprised.

"I know, except we won't be in Moonlight Falls when I give it to her," Emma said, looking sad. "Besides, I don't know how to wrap my present."

"Hmm," said Dr. Chris. He bent over to be at Emma's eye level and spoke directly to her. "I'm pretty good at wrapping Christmas presents, so maybe I could help you wrap it before you leave today."

"That would be great!"

# CHAPTER 21

SNOW HAD FALLEN throughout the morning and into the afternoon on Christmas Eve Day, leaving a thick, white blanket covering everything in Moonlight Falls. Molly looked out her kitchen window and found herself struggling to enjoy the beauty outside without remembering what had happened exactly one year ago to the day when a similar snowstorm had caused the roads to become dangerously icy. Molly looked at the clock above the sink. It read 1:34. An hour and half earlier, Will had left to take Annie and Molly to the airport. His plan was to wait there until Jake's plane arrived, then drive home with his Army buddy in tow and arrive in time for the family's traditional Secret Santa party.

Walking nervously around the kitchen, Molly was on pins and needles waiting for Will to call, or at least text her, saying they had arrived safely at the airport. After looking into the oven for the fiftieth time, she could not restrain herself. She picked up her cell phone and tapped a short text message to Will: **On your way home?**

After a few minutes of waiting for her cell to ping with Will's response, Molly walked to the stove and began to stir the Taylor family's Christmas Eve favorite, *froot-ta-sooppa*. It was simmering exactly as it should, so she turned the flame down and covered the large kettle. *Maybe Will couldn't text back because he'd just dropped Annie and Emma off at the airport curbside,* thought Molly. *Or maybe he was caught in the airport congestion as he looked for a parking space. Or maybe Will was already at the baggage claim area, waiting for his buddy to arrive.* It also occurred to Molly that maybe her text didn't go through, given the unpredictability of some cell zones. *Or maybe Will's friend Jake had just arrived and the two of them were in the midst of greeting each other.* Molly convinced herself that any one of these reasons would explain why Will had not yet responded to her text.

"Hello, hello," Jenny called from the foyer. She closed the front door with her foot to keep the cold outside.

Molly wiped her hands on her apron and scurried from kitchen to the front door to help Jenny with the two platters she held in her arms.

"Oh, my, what have you brought this Christmas?" From the moment Molly kissed Jenny on the cheek, she sensed that her daughter was on edge and unexpectedly reserved. Something was wrong, so Molly looked around. "Where's Sam?"

"Oh, um, he's coming a little later, Mom." Jenny handed one of her trays to Molly and then marched toward the kitchen. "By the way, Mom, Sam and I were wondering if we should wait until after Annie and Emma return from Orlando to open the Secret Santa presents. It doesn't seem right without Emma and Annie here."

"I don't know," said Molly with a sigh. "Annie and Emma came over last night and put a little gift under the tree. Emma said it was her Secret Santa gift for me, and she made me promise that I would open it at exactly four o'clock today."

Jenny smiled knowing Emma had picked four o'clock because that had always been the hour when the family gathered for their Secret Santa exchange. This allowed enough time before leaving for the early Christmas Eve service at their church.

"I promised Emma that Grandpa would take a picture of me when I opened it," said Molly. "Annie wants him to send it to her phone so Emma can see it when they land in Orlando. We should at least open *that* Secret Santa gift."

"That's so sweet. Of course, you have to open that one," said Jenny.

Molly knew Jenny loved Emma as if she were her own daughter, a bond that had grown even stronger over the past year.

Jenny looked around the kitchen and inhaled the sweet smell of the fruit soup. "Mom, it smells so good in here." She lifted the lid of the slow cooker to catch a glimpse of Molly's famous Christmas Raspberry Glazed Ham that, year after year, Molly had perfectly timed to be ready the moment the family returned home from church. "What can I do to help?" asked Jenny.

"Everything's about ready."

"Well, let me set the table," said Jenny, overly eager to stay out of Molly's way.

Molly looked at her daughter, sensing her anxiety. This past week Jenny had kept her phone calls with Molly short and somewhat edgy and, most telling of all, she'd said she was too busy to join Molly, Annie and Emma and at their traditional Christmas High Tea at the Moonlight Falls Tea House.

"Is everything okay with you and Sam?" Molly didn't want to pry, but she was also worried that something was very wrong between Jenny and Sam. They'd had a difficult couple of years trying to start a family, but until now, Sam and Jenny had been strong and supportive of each other. Molly was worried that the disappointment and stress of all the miscarriages was tearing them apart.

When Jenny didn't answer, Molly retreated to the living room to adjust some of the ornaments on the tree. She thought it best to let Jenny set the table alone.

Bill had been in the backyard gathering some firewood, unaware of Jenny's arrival. He walked into the back porch mudroom with a pile of firewood in his arms, shook off the snow, stomped his feet and walked into the kitchen. Jenny was sorting through the silverware drawer and looked up.

"Hey!" Bill gave Jenny a big smile, happy to see her at the house so early. Still holding the firewood, he leaned over to kiss her cheek.

"Merry Christmas, Dad," Jenny said without kissing him in return. "You'd better put those logs down before you wrench your arm." Jenny didn't look at her father. Instead, she walked away with a handful of forks and spoons.

Bill cocked his head to the side, puzzled by the cool greeting from his usually effusive daughter. He shrugged it off, placed the firewood in a canvas sling and carried the logs into the living room.

As Bill entered the room, he watched Molly absentmindedly moving ornaments from one branch of the Christmas tree to another, then suddenly change her mind only to return the same ornament to its original spot.

"Where's Sam?" Bill asked as he bent down beside the fireplace.

Molly turned around, surprised to see her husband. "Jenny says he'll be coming a little later."

"Oh?" Bill stood up, and the moment he saw the worry in Molly's face, he walked over to her and put his arms around her. They held each other in silence. "We knew this was would be a difficult Christmas."

Molly nodded, then nestled her head into Bill's chest. "Oh Bill, how can it be that Annie and Emma are struggling so hard to make life work without Ron? How can it be that our son has suffered such a terrible, debilitating injury? And why, oh why, aren't Jenny and Sam able to have a child?"

"Why is the love of my life fighting cancer?" Bill whispered into Molly's ear. Unexpectedly, the front door opened. Molly and Bill looked up and watched Sam step into the foyer. "Sorry I'm late," Sam called out before closing the door. He stomped on the area rug to shake the snow from his shoes.

"Sam!" Molly cried. "Oh, I'm so happy you're here!" Molly rushed from the living room to give her son-in-law a hug.

"Me, too," Sam said, perplexed by Molly's overly solicitous greeting.

Jenny had heard the sound of her husband's greeting just as she had completed setting the dinner table. She took a deep breath, then left the dining room to join her parents and Sam.

Molly had released Sam from her embrace but was still hovering near him as if not wanting to let him out of her sight.

"Ah, so, um, is Will back from taking Annie and Emma to the airport?" asked Sam.

"We haven't heard from him yet," said Molly.

Bill looked at his watch. It was almost four o'clock. "He probably won't be here for another hour, given the weather."

Jenny nodded at Sam, barely smiling at him. The four of them stood still, knowing that the memory of last year's Christmas Eve had been permanently engraved into each of their minds.

Bill gently clapped his hands and rubbed them together in an attempt to break the spell. "Molly, how's the *froo-ta-soopa* doing? Shouldn't we be having a cup of it with a Christmas toast by now?"

The sound of Bill's voice and his words were just what was needed to break through their moment of sorrow, causing everyone to join in a spontaneous group hug. After holding each other for a long time, they walked arm in arm into the dining room to share a cup of their traditional Christmas Eve cheer. Almost reverently, the four of them sat quietly at the table for a few moments sipping the fruit soup.

Sam broke the silence. "I look forward to this every year," he said before taking a big sip of the hot soup. As Jenny, Molly and Bill joined him in another sip of the Christmas drink, the chimes of the grandfather clock announced that it was four o'clock.

"Oh my!" Molly jumped from her chair. "I've got to open Emma's Secret Santa gift! And Bill, get your cell phone camera ready. Remember, Emma told you to take a picture and send it to her." Molly put her napkin on the table and nervously walked into the living room, followed by Sam, Jenny and Bill.

Everyone watched as Molly reached for the gift under the tree and untied the ribbon. She opened the rectangular box and removed a piece of paper with a crayon-drawn picture of a child holding out both arms. Printed in red and green letters were the words *Happy Secret Santa, Grandma*. Molly smiled and showed the drawing to the others in the room, and then Bill held up his cell phone to take a picture of Molly smiling and holding Emma's present to her heart.

The doorbell rang before he had time to take another picture. Molly looked toward the front door, relieved at knowing Will had finally arrived home safely. As she walked to the entryway, Molly had a momentary flashback to last Christmas Eve, when Bill had opened the door hoping to see Ron and Annie and Emma.

She stopped in her tracks just for an instant, looked back at Bill, Jenny and Sam, then moved forward and opened the door, joyfully anticipating seeing Will and his friend, Jake.

"Merry Christmas Eve! Happy Secret Santa Present!"

Every muscle in Molly's body stood frozen in place. On the front porch sat Emma in her wheelchair and Annie, standing behind her, holding onto the wheelchair handles. Molly squealed, threw her arms wide open and then rushed to hug Emma. Still bent over, she looked up at Annie. "I thought Will took you to the airport."

Emma laughed and said, "Uncle Willy went to pick up his

friend Jake at the airport and bring him home for Christmas Eve before Santa gets here." Emma couldn't contain her joy at having pulled off such a big surprise.

Jenny, Sam and Bill joined them on the front porch where everyone hugged and kissed Emma and Annie. After several more minutes of warm, loving embraces, while still standing in the freezing cold, Bill helped wheel his granddaughter into the Christmas Eve warmth of the Taylor home.

Jenny stared at Annie, perplexed. "How did you get here without your car?"

Annie looked toward the driveway and watched Dr. Chris close his car door and walk up the front steps carrying an armful of Christmas presents.

Jenny looked at Annie with a grin, her eyebrows raised as if waiting for an explanation.

"Don't get any ideas. He's just dropping us off," Annie mumbled quietly to her sister.

"Uncle Willy still had to go to the airport to get his buddy, so he asked Dr. Chris to bring Mommy and me here," explained Emma, finishing with a satisfied, Cheshire cat smile for the whole room to see.

Dr. Chris stepped into the foyer and handed an armful of presents to Sam.

"Dr. Chris," rang out Molly, still glowing with the excitement that her whole family would be home for Christmas. "Can you stay for a cup of fruit soup?"

"Well, if you insist," said Dr. Chris to Molly, whose expectant look gave him no choice. "I've heard it's awesome."

Annie looked at Dr. Chris, and for just a fleeting second, she wondered if this was a good idea.

# CHAPTER 22

THE SHOCK AND joy of seeing Annie and Emma sitting in the living room near the Christmas tree on Christmas Eve along with Bill, Jenny and Sam—and Dr. Chris—was enough to subdue the worry Molly felt inside, but it didn't stop her from offering several short, silent prayers asking for Will's safe trip home as he drove through the winter storm. *Please God, bring my son home safely.*

Emma had been so thrilled with Annie's and her Secret Santa surprise that she could not help herself from giggling and saying over and over, "We really surprised you, didn't we?"

"Yes, you did, you silly girl, and you've given us the very best Christmas present ever." Molly handed a cup of warm fruit soup to her granddaughter and kissed her on the cheek.

Molly looked up when she heard the front door open and close.

"Have you started without me?" came Will's voice from the entryway.

"Will!" Molly rushed to help him take off his coat. "Now everyone is here safe and sound." Molly instantly wished she could reel those words back into her mouth, as she not only felt the pain of her *faux pas*, but she immediately knew the wrenching impact those words had on Annie. Her beloved Ron was not there. *Everyone was not here safe and sound.*

"But Grandma, not everybody is here," Emma said.

The room fell silent with the weight of her words.

Emma looked at her uncle. "Uncle Willy, where is your buddy?"

"Oh, Emma, I'm glad you asked." Will looked down at his niece and his face showed serious concern. "My buddy Jake is here but—"

"But what?" Emma asked, looking troubled.

"But he's very shy and kind of needs someone other than me to ask him to come inside. I was hoping you could talk him into joining us," said Will as he stood in the doorway, looking into the living room.

Emma's face lit up and without a word she wheeled herself over to the front door. Will stepped forward and opened the door wide.

"Ohhhhhhh," was all Emma said as she looked outside.

Everyone rushed over to the entry hallway so they, too, could look out the door and see what Emma was seeing.

A large, silent and very handsome German Shepherd was sitting at attention at the bottom of the steps between the two Steadfast Christmas Soldiers. He was staring at the group, his tail wagging as snow landed gently on his fur. His red tongue hung to the right side of his mouth and his pointed ears stood straight up in the air. He was panting ever so slightly while his posture suggested he was seated in a ready-for-action position, waiting for a command.

Emma looked at her uncle with tears welling in her eyes. "Is he your buddy, Jake?"

"Yes, Emma. This is my best buddy, Jake."

Emma turned her attention back to the front porch. "Hello, Jake."

"He won't come inside unless you say, 'Jake, come'," Will told Emma.

"Jake, come," said Emma, holding out her arms as she watched the dog stand up and hobble up the steps. It was then that Emma noticed the dog was missing his left hind leg.

"Oh, Jake!" Emma hugged the dog's neck as he licked her face.

"Emmabanemma," Will said softly and with much love in his voice. "Jake's had lots of physical therapy and now he can walk and run as well as any dog."

"Oh, Jake, I'm going to be just like you," Emma looked into Jake's brown eyes. "I'm going to walk and run someday too."

"The thing is, Emma," said Will as he stroked Jake's back, "Jake is retired from the Army because of his injury, and he doesn't have a home to go to, so I was hoping that you and your mom might give him a home."

Emma immediately looked at Annie with a yearning that could not be denied.

"Emmy," Annie said softly. "Uncle Willy already asked me if we could have Jake and—"

"Mommy, please!"

Bill, Molly, Jenny, Sam and Dr. Chris looked as if they were holding their collective breath.

"And I told him we'd love to have Jake in our family." Annie smiled at her daughter.

Suddenly, the small foyer with the garland of white twinkling lights draped along the stairwell filled with bursts of cheers and laughter. Jake lifted his chin from Emma's lap and let out a low howl as if he, too, were cheering.

"Is Jake my Secret Santa gift?" asked Emma with tears still streaming down her cheeks. She looked at Will and the instant he nodded his head, Emma squealed in a six-year-old's joyful, ecstatic voice. "Jake, you are the best Secret Santa present ever!"

There was more laughter and lots of hugs around the doorway. Bill looked at his watch. "Hey everyone, if we're going to make it to church on time, we'd better get started on the rest of the Secret Santa presents." He ushered everyone back into the living room.

# CHAPTER 23

ONCE EVERYONE WAS settled in the living room, Molly noticed the tension between Jenny and Sam as they sat stiffly beside each other on the sofa. She remembered that Jenny had not wanted to open the Secret Santa gifts on Christmas Eve. *But wasn't that because Annie and Emma wouldn't be here?* Molly gave Jenny an inquisitive look wondering if she should still delay the gift-giving. Jenny, of course, understood the nonverbal communication from her mother and returned her mother's look with a reassuring smile, a signal that it would be okay to open the gifts that night after all.

"Okay, let's see," said Bill, rubbing his hands together in mock expectation. "Annie gave *her* Secret Santa, Will gave *his* Secret Santa, so who's going to be next?" Bill bent down and picked up one of the gift boxes that Sam had brought in earlier. "Well, this one says, For Mom and Dad." Bill tilted his head to his left then to his right as if analyzing the size of the gift box. "Hmmm. Emma, this looks pretty small compared to the size of your Secret Santa gift."

Emma laughed and hugged Jake who was seated beside her wheelchair. "I love you, Jake," said Emma.

"And this one definitely isn't as big as the package you and your mom brought," said Bill. He walked over to Molly and handed her the square box wrapped in bright red and green wrapping paper, tied with a simple ribbon. "Molly, I'll let you open it."

Molly reached for the box and looked around the room trying to remember who had brought the gift. She slowly tore the paper from the box, looked at it for a moment, then held it up. "Bill, since this is for both of us, *you* should open it."

Bill stepped closer to his wife and lifted the lid off the box. He removed the tissue paper and looked inside, staring for a long moment before pulling a tiny pair of blue socks from the box. He looked inside again and then pulled out a tiny pair of pink socks. Perplexed, holding a pair of socks in each hand, Bill looked at Molly, and with their mouths wide open, they began looking around the room for an explanation. Together they stopped and stared at Jenny and Sam, who were smiling and nodding their heads in the affirmative.

"We just found out a few days ago, and it's been so hard to keep it a secret." Jenny began to cry.

"Oh, Jenny," Molly sighed with relief. "Is that why you were so short with me whenever I called?"

Jenny nodded through her tears, then composed herself. "I'm so sorry, but I knew if I talked with you or Annie for very long, I wouldn't be able to wait for Christmas Eve to tell you."

In unison Molly and Annie screamed, and Bill, Will and Dr. Chris cheered as Jenny and Sam stood up to receive everyone's hugs.

"Hey, what is going on?" Emma shouted above all the noise and commotion.

Jenny stepped closer to Emma and leaned down. She gently held onto Emma's shoulders. "Emmy, you are going to have a girl cousin and a boy cousin this spring," Jenny whispered. The two hugged tightly until Jake nuzzled his head between them.

"Did you hear that, Jake?" asked Emma, as everyone in the room laughed out loud.

Molly looked around the room at her happy family, almost as if looking at them from above, and her heart melted. She wanted to preserve the moment in her mind, to memorize it for posterity. After a few seconds, she got up and walked to the Christmas tree. She looked around and then reached for a present. "Well, let's see. It looks like almost everyone has given a Secret Santa except me."

"And me," Bill laughed.

"You'll just have to wait!" said Molly, with comedic authority. She walked around the room as if having a hard time finding the right person to give the present to until she finally arrived where her husband was sitting. "This one says it's for you."

Bill looked at the rectangular box and shook it. "Looks awfully thin, and it's as light as a feather. I hope it's not one of those ugly Christmas ties." He handed the gift box to Emma. "What do you think Emma?"

Emma shook the box just as her grandfather had done.

"I think it's an empty box, Grandpa. Maybe your Secret Santa present is invisible." Emma giggled and handed the box back over to her grandfather.

"Well, then it will remain a secret, won't it?" He laughed along with his family. "Okay, let's just find out."

Bill removed the paper and ribbon, lifted the top of the box and looked inside. He tilted his head to the side, slowly lifted out an eight by eleven sheet of paper and began to silently read its contents. Seconds later Bill looked up at his wife to see that she was smiling at him.

"Yes?" He appeared to be filled with emotional pain. He stood up, and Molly did, too.

"Yes." Molly wrapped her arms around Bill's neck, and as they held each other, everyone in the room could see they were both in tears, swaying slightly as if holding each other up.

The crackling sound of burning wood in the fireplace and the low, gentle chords of Christmas music playing from the speakers was all anyone could hear. Bill looked at his children, and seeing how worried they all looked, he held up the piece of paper, cleared his throat and began to read out loud. "Test results for Molly Taylor: CEA 124, negative. HE4: negative. Diagnosis: Full remission of cancer."

Once again, the Taylor home was filled with the grateful sound of cheers and applause, and once again there were more tears and hugs all around until even Jake started howling. It took quite a while for all the excitement and joy to settle down and allow them to bask in the pure joy of the moment.

"Grandpa!" Emma said with urgency. "Will gave a Secret Santa, Mommy gave a Secret Santa, and Aunt Jenny and Uncle Sam gave a Secret Santa, and so did Grandma, but you haven't given one yet."

"Oh, how could I forget! Well, okay then." Bill reached for a present the size of a shoe box and handed it to Molly who quickly tore off the paper and opened it.

"Well, what in the world is this?" Molly looked up at Bill.

"It's confetti. It's Christmas confetti for everyone!" Bill dipped his fingers into the box and sprinkled some of the tiny flecks of paper on his wife's head. Then he proceeded to walk around the room, sprinkling the Christmas confetti on top of everyone else's head, leading to more laughter and giggles, even though, judging by their puzzled looks, nobody understood the significance of the confetti.

"Bill Taylor," Molly laughed, "you are one strange man."

"I like confetti!" Emma shouted and threw tiny white and black pieces of paper into the air, some of which landed on Jake's back and head. "But Grandpa, shouldn't Christmas confetti be red and green?"

"Oh, that's a good point, Emma. But, you see, this is very special Christmas confetti."

Complete silence and stares of confusion converged upon Bill who had a quixotic, bemused look on his face. He picked up another handful of the tiny pieces of paper and threw them high into the air.

"These confetti pieces were made from the sales contract and escrow papers for our house."

More silence.

"I cancelled the deal. The Taylor home is no longer for sale!" Bill bellowed.

Molly screamed and jumped up and down while hugging Bill. Of course, everyone else in the room did the same. It took quite a while for the family to once again regain their collective composure, but when calm was finally restored, Emma announced loudly, "Dr. Chris, you're the only one left to give a Secret Santa."

"Oh, Emma, no one expects that of Dr. Chris," said Annie quickly, embarrassed that Emma would put him on the spot regarding a tradition he knew nothing about.

The doctor smiled at Emma as if he had not been put on the spot.

"Actually, I do have a gift, but I won't be able to give it without your help, Emma," said Dr. Chris as he stood up and wheeled Emma closer to the Christmas tree.

"Which one should I pick?" Dr. Chris asked.

Emma pointed to one of the boxes he had carried in earlier. "That one," she said to the doctor.

He bent down and reached for a box wrapped in red and gold paper, tied with green ribbon. It obviously had not been wrapped by an amateur wrapper.

"Secret Santa for Annie. That's you, Mommy!" said Emma, smiling at her mom just as Dr. Chris walked the gift to over to where Annie was seated.

"For me?" Annie was surprised. *How was it that Dr. Chris had a Secret Santa gift and why in the world was he giving it to her?* She certainly didn't think to give him a Christmas gift. Well, except for the green coffee mug with the words Dr. Chris glazed on it. But that was from Emma to him, not from Annie to Dr. Chris.

"Hurry up, Mommy."

Annie opened the box and peered inside. She looked up at Emma and Dr. Chris and laughed. "Oh, you two! I think I'd better tell everyone your joke before I show them my gift."

"Yes!" Emma couldn't contain herself. "Tell the joke."

"Well, you see," Annie paused to look at everyone, "a while back Dr. Chris told Emma that her brain was trying to send messages to her legs."

"And guess what I told Dr. Chris?" Emma interrupted.

"What?" Will, Jenny, Sam and Molly and Bill all asked at the same time.

"I told Dr. Chris that I thought my legs needed hearing aids!" Emma giggled at her own joke and then watched as her entire family did the same thing.

"Mommy, show them!"

Annie looked at Dr. Chris and when their eyes met, Annie saw him wink at her, a twinkle in his eyes. Unintentionally, Annie gave a slight wink in return before she pulled out two very large and very antiquated hearing aids from the box. Holding them between her thumbs and pointer fingers, Annie held them high enough for all to see. Nervous laughter filled the room. "What in the world?" asked Molly, staring at the devices as they were passed around the room for everyone to see.

Together Emma and Dr. Chris watched as the hearing aids

were cheerfully passed around the room. No one really noticed that Dr. Chris had slowly walked over to Emma, knelt down beside the wheelchair and carefully attached thin cables to two patches on her thighs. Eventually, one by one, Molly, Bill, Will, Jenny, Sam and Annie stopped what they were doing to look at Emma and Dr. Chris.

If a pin had fallen to the floor, it would have shattered the silence. Dr. Chris and Emma smiled at each other and nodded in agreement. Emma pointed to the hearing aids Annie was once again holding in her hands.

"Well, guess what. Those hearing aids don't help my legs to hear my brain."

The room was silent for another very long moment.

"But this hearing aid does." Emma held up a keypad the size of a paperback book. She pressed a button and looked down at her leg. She produced a deep inhale, then quietly said, "Left thigh, going up."

Every eye in the room was fixated on Emma and on her leg.

Emma looked up at Dr. Chris, who nodded, then looked again at her left leg. She repeated for all to hear, "Left thigh, going up." And then, the most miraculous thing happened before their very eyes: Emma's left thigh rose from the wheelchair.

Annie's hands covered her mouth to hold down a choking sound.

"Left leg going down," Emma grunted. Her left leg dropped beside her right leg.

The Taylor house filled with cheers.

"Wait!" Emma held up her hands. Instantly, the room became silent. Emma looked at her right leg. "Right thigh, going up." And miracle of miracles, Emma's right thigh rose ever so slightly from the seat of the wheelchair just as her left thigh had done a moment ago.

Annie's eyes darted back and forth between Emma's thighs and Dr. Chris's face, as she searched for an explanation. Dr. Chris smiled at Annie, then gave one of his signature winks. Immediately, tears came streaming down Annie's cheeks as she rushed over to her daughter and hugged her with all her might.

"Happy Secret Santa, Mommy."

# CHAPTER 24

MOONLIGHT FALLS COMMUNITY Church had never looked as glorious as it did on this Christmas Eve. Three pine trees trimmed with tiny white lights stood on each side of the altar, a row of bright red poinsettia lined the railing that separated the sanctuary from the nave, and the colors of the eight stained glass windows on each side of the church flickered from lighted candles sitting on their windowsills. Overhead lights were dimmed, allowing the congregants to bask in the warm glow of candlelight.

The thirty-five choir members, dressed in deep maroon and gold-colored robes, had formed a line in the vestibule quietly waiting for their cue to begin the processional song. The church was filled to capacity with families and friends from Moonlight Falls all greeting each other with hugs and kisses, waving to each other from across the sanctuary and whispering happy salutations.

The pipe organ suddenly sounded with a prelude and began to fill the sanctuary with the familiar strands of "Joy to the World." The choir began their processional march singing the glorious old standard, joined now as the full congregation stood in place and added their voices to the song. As if beckoned from the heavens above, a magnificent spirit of joy filled every corner of the church.

As the choir members reached their places up front, the minister walked the final steps up to the altar, then turned to face the worshipers as together they sang the last stanza of the hymn:

*He rules the world, with truth and grace,*
*and makes the nations prove,*
*the glories of his righteousness*
*and wonders of his love...*

At that moment, an usher led Bill and Molly Taylor down the center aisle to the front pew, Jenny and Sam right behind them, followed by Will, hobbling on his crutches. Next, Annie entered the sanctuary, followed by Dr. Chris pushing Emma in her wheelchair. Led down the aisle by a second usher, Annie then took her place beside Will and watched as Dr. Chris gently lifted Emma from the wheelchair, placed her on the pew next to Annie and then squeezed in beside Emma. The usher took the wheelchair away as the choir and congregation sang the final words of the hymn.

*And wonders of His love,*
*And wonders, wonders of His love.*

"Merry Christmas, everyone," shouted the minister from the pulpit.

"Merry Christmas!" came the loud, boisterous response from everyone in the congregation.

"Welcome to Moonlight Falls Community Church." The minister paused to absorb the beauty of the moment and to let everyone get settled back into their seats.

In the front row, Emma quietly reached for Annie's hand and gently placed it in her lap. And then, just as gently, she reached for Dr. Chris's hand and placed it over Annie's. Annie and Dr.

Chris looked down at Emma's lap and watched as Emma added her own hands to theirs. Emma did not look at either of them as she did this. She just smiled an angelic smile and looked straight ahead at the altar where the choir and the minister were standing. Dr. Chris and Annie looked at each other with smiles filled with warmth and wonder... the smiles of two people who were slowly but surely falling in love.

The minister stretched his arms out wide and addressed his congregation. "What a blessing it is to be together here in Moonlight Falls on this snowy Christmas Eve where the mysterious forces of strength and faith, hope and love are very much alive."

# About Trish Evans

Trish Evans is the author of *Katy's Ghost,* a fictional memoir, and *The Mom Prom Murder,* the first of a series of cozy mysteries under the banner of **The Berger and Fryze Mysteries.** She was born and raised in Southern California in an eccentric family of journalists, writers and musicians. She graduated from Northwestern University in Evanston, Illinois. When not tapping on her keyboard, Trish can usually be found working in her garden, riding her bicycle or walking along the sandy shores of Malibu with Ollie, a goldendoodle. She's married to her college sweetheart. They live in southern California and spend as much time at the beach as possible.

Visit her at trishevansbooks.com.

Made in the USA
Monee, IL
24 November 2020

49462831R00090